The Sunday Doll

Books by Mary Francis Shura

The Sunday Doll
Don't Call Me Toad!
The Josie Gambit
The Search for Grissi
Happles and Cinnamunger
The Barkley Street Six-pack
Mister Wolf and Me
The Gray Ghosts of Taylor Ridge
The Riddle of Raven's Gulch

and the companion books

Chester
Eleanor
Jefferson

The Sunday Doll

Mary Francis Shura

DODD, MEAD & COMPANY   New York

Library of Congress Cataloging-in-Publication Data

Shura, Mary Francis.
    The Sunday doll / Mary Francis Shura.
    p.   cm.
    Summary: Thirteen-year-old Emmy finds herself sheltered again from
her family's problems when she is hastily sent to Aunt Harriett's for
the summer because of a serious problem involving her older sister
Jayne.
    ISBN 0-396-09309-4
    [1. Family problems—Fiction.]   I. Title.
PZ7.S55983Su   1988   88-3586
[Fic]—dc19   CIP
                                                        AC

To Ali, the Monday Doll,
with complete love

Contents

The
Sunday Doll

1
Special Delivery

No girl who has won a red ribbon in a Science Fair should admit to being superstitious, so I don't. But the strange and scary things that happened during my birthday week *seemed* to begin when my present from Aunt Harriet arrived in my life.

It was Sunday, the seventh of June, with my birthday coming up on Tuesday. Already I knew there were both good and bad things about the coming week. The good thing was that, when school let out on Friday, I would get to go visit my Aunt Harriett in Missouri. The bad thing was that, no matter how much I hated the idea, I would turn thirteen on my birthday. More than anything in the world, I didn't want to be a teenager.

A little while after lunch, the postman pulled into our drive with a special delivery package. Only my parents and I were home because my sister, Jayne, was out with her wimp of a boyfriend, Geoff Wheaton, and my brother, Derek, had gone into Chicago to a Cubs' game with a bunch of his friends.

I was on the front steps brushing our dog, Murph. Murph the Mutt, while appearing to be a black lab, is actually a living, hairy bundle of clichés. He barks at the moon, buries bones in flowerbeds, and chases mailmen.

The minute I saw the truck, I grabbed Murph's collar and braced myself. Before the thing even stopped, Murph had bared his teeth in a snarl and was choking himself, trying to lunge down the sidewalk toward the driver.

Dad, who had been mowing the lawn, shut the motor off. "Hang on to him, Emmy," he called to me. "I'll sign for it."

[If that scene had been in a movie, the background music would have dropped to a lower key and begun to sound ominous. The cameras would have zoomed in on Dad signing the green card and holding the package.]

Instead, everything was business as usual in

sunny suburbia. The air was thick with the pungent green smell of freshly cut grass and the sounds of Dad and the postman shouting at each other, above Murph's barking, as they bewailed the Cubs' prospects for the season.

But then, if that whole week had been a movie, I could have understood what was happening. Making people understand what's going on is the business of a moviemaker. Since this was real life instead of changing lights projected against a screen, I had to cope with a lot of other painful feelings— anger, frustration, confusion, and an aching kind of loneliness.

I first realized something was wrong when I went inside to put the package from Aunt Harriett on the hall table. Because I was a little blinded from the sun outside, I almost ran into Mom, who was standing beside the phone in the hall. She didn't look like herself. She was very still, as if she were holding her breath and thinking sad thoughts.

"Mom!" I cried. "What's the matter? Is something wrong?"

If they presented awards for skill at giving double signals, my mom would be a gold medal winner. She caught a little sob in her throat, making it plain that something *was* wrong, and spoke to me in a bright, cheery tone.

"Of course not, Emmy!" she said. Then, after hesitating only a moment, she smiled, showing me more teeth than anyone needed to see except maybe our dentist. She touched my arm. "Would you tell Dad I want to speak with him?"

I stared at her, careful not to let my annoyance show in my face. Nothing irritates me more about my parents than the way they always act as if everything is fine when it obviously isn't. Do they really think that a pat on the head, a blinding smile, and a lilting voice can turn off a kid's brain like a water faucet? As much as I hated the fact that my birthday was going to make me a teenager, maybe when I got that "teen" on the end of my age, they would quit treating me this way.

She stared back at me, so deep in thought that she didn't even realize I was still there. When she came to, she spoke again, sharpening her tone just a tad. "Please, Emmy," she said. "Don't just stand there staring at me with that closed look on your face. I asked you to take a message to your father."

I turned away, angry and resentful. I had as much right to hide my feelings from her as she did to shut me out of everything and treat me like a child.

It's no wonder that I like movies better than I do real life. As I said, moviemakers work hard to keep you informed of what's going on. Your family and friends put just as much effort into keeping you in the dark. And because moviemakers aren't very sure how smart you are, they provide wonderful signals to warn you of what is coming—the camera moves in close as if to say: "Look at this! Now *this* means trouble!"

The grownups in my family conceal all their concerns under a careful flurry of business as usual. The sky could be falling in big chunks, thundering down on our roof like meteorites, and Mom would still insist that we eat nutritious meals on time. The Thing That Ate New York could be crossing the lake on its way to Chicago and Dad would ask all three of us about our homework. It could be written in the sky that tomorrow had been canceled and the two of them would gang up on me to make sure that I got to bed on time and missed the old rerun movie I had been waiting forever to see. Jayne and Derek are no help. It's no good trying to pump them about what's going on because they joined forces with Mom and Dad when they became teenagers.

But Mom and Dad end up by outfoxing themselves. They are so dependable that, when they make any break in the pattern, I know there's trouble. Right away I begin to panic from not knowing what is wrong under all that sweetness and light. It was so unlike Mom to stand in a dark hall with her mascara softened and her mouth bleak that I began to shiver inside.

When I got outdoors, the postal truck was gone, Murph was asleep on the steps, and Dad was mowing again, overlapping the rows so that, by the time he reached the hedge, the yard would look like a golf green, with no stripes anywhere. I ran alongside a few feet before he noticed me and looked over. I played a game I think of as Marcel the Mime. I signaled him to go into the house, moving my mouth wide but not making any sound because he wouldn't be able to hear me anyway. He looked puzzled a moment, then turned the mower down to a slow, coughing mutter. "I didn't get that," he told me.

"Mom wants to see you."

He measured the distance to the end of the row with his eyes and made a frowning guess as to how many rows were left to do. "What about?" he asked.

I wanted to ask him when anyone had ever told me the reason for anything. But, instead, I shook my head. "She just asked me to get you."

He sighed, then looked at me thoughtfully.

14

"You think you could run this thing for a minute?" he asked.

Nodding, I reached for the handles. Another breakthrough. I had been trying to get my hands on that mower for the entire two years since I mistakenly let it cut the spears off a whole line of gladiolus just ready to bloom. Parents may forgive, but they never forget.

I finished that row singing at the top of my lungs, because a mower makes even more noise than a shower. I did the next row and hesitated just a second. I was nervous about the last row, but I kept going and made it clear to the end without a casualty in Mom's blooming border. By that time, little rivers of sweat were streaming down my spine and my hair was wet enough to stick to my shoulders. Little jagged threads of mowed grass had pasted themselves to my legs and turned my skin green.

Dad was still in the house but he must have heard me turn the mower off because he came out on the porch.

"Good job, Emmy!" he said in that hearty tone I really hate because he only uses it to me. "How about a matinee this afternoon?"

I was naturally struck dumb. It's no secret that I like movies better than anyone except the people who act in them. But this was my dad talking—my dad, who nags at me all the time for sitting in front of a TV movie when I could be enjoying the glorious out-of-doors. Was he really suggesting we go to an afternoon show?

"Well, what about it?" he pressed. "I'll pay."

This was getting scary. The movie was strange enough, but not to have to pay for it out of my allowance was unbelievable.

"What are we going to see?" I asked, because he was waiting so eagerly.

His face looked funny. "I'm not going," he said. "I thought maybe you and Cassie would like to take one in together."

I waited for him to say more. So far this hadn't made sense. Neither he nor Mom had ever come right out and said they didn't like my best friend, Cassie Malone, but I knew very well they didn't. Not that I blamed them. Cassie can be totally ridiculous without even knowing it, and she lapses into obnoxious when she works on it. Not only is she the world's worst show-off, but she says awful things about people unless you yell at her and just refuse to listen. I probably couldn't stand her myself except I know her so well that she never surprises me. Besides, she's the only *close* friend I've ever had, and I miss her even if we have a short fight. "Did she call?" I asked, starting up the steps.

He reached out and hooked his arm lightly around my neck. "I called her," he said, in that kind of country-western drawl that he puts on when he's kidding me. "She allowed as how she'd love to see what's showing at Oakbrook Center and have a sandwich with you at the French Baker's before coming home."

When you have really worked up a sweat, your skin gets cold when a breeze hits it. That was the logical explanation for the chilly way I felt under the warmth of his arm. "We've both seen that one," I told him.

He chuckled. "When did that ever keep you two away from a movie? Get changed fast. I'll take you up there, and Mrs. Malone will pick you up when you call."

"Why can't you pick us up?" I asked him.

"Emmy," he reproached me, only half play-fully. "Is there some reason you don't want to do this?"

What was I going to say? I could hardly ask him if this was the first move in one of those crazy games he and Mom have played before with Jayne and Derek and me. Maybe I forgive and don't for-get, too. I definitely remember that we were prac-tically packed for the move from Connecticut to Chicago before I happened to find out that Dad had lost his job three months earlier and had been going on interviews to get a new job instead of going to the office.

But this was more than keeping secrets from me. He was shipping me off. I almost asked him where the big bag of candy was, but I wasn't sure he'd realize what I meant.

To me, being shipped off always has ended with my getting to pick out a big bag of candy. It took years for me to understand *Snow White* because Mom led me out to the movie lobby to select candy while the witch poisoned that apple. I spent the last half of *Oliver* trying to figure out what happened to the girl because of a sack of gummy bears Mom let me buy during her murder. I *still* don't know what happened to Bambi because that movie never comes back on reruns.

I shrugged and shook my head. Dad checked his watch again and held the front door open for me. The air conditioner sighed and began to blow softly.

It was hot even for Chicago in early June, but I shivered as I walked into the hall. On the way upstairs, I picked up the package I had set on the hall table and shook it, before putting it back down. The shape of the package, like an oversized shoe box, and the way something slid heavily inside, confirmed my worst suspicions. Aunt Harriett had sent me another birthday doll! I groaned, wishing the postman had taken the package instead of the green card back with him. I know one is supposed to be grateful for presents and I usually am. But the last thing I needed in the world was *another* doll.

I probably have one of the best doll collections of any kid in the Chicago area. Strangely, I don't really like any of them very much, even though most of them came from Aunt Harriett, whom I love with all my heart.

I tried to wipe the green grass stain off my legs, but, when it only smudged, I took a fast shower and thought about how great it would be to be back on the farm with Aunt Harriett and Aaron.

Aunt Harriett is really my father's great aunt, which means she is his grandmother's sister, or would be except that his grandmother died a long time ago. She is older than anyone else I know, and is different from the old people in my friends' families. Their old relatives either live across town somewhere and ask them over for holiday dinners or have condominiums in Florida where the kids get to visit and play on the beach a couple of times a year.

Our Aunt Harriett lives on a cliff above the

Mississippi River in a huge house that is so old it makes strange noises all by itself. The place is crammed with memories for Aunt Harriett. She talks about long ago relatives as if their spirits hadn't left when they died but, instead, still linger in the house, playing the piano or walking the halls the way they used to do. I love it there, and every year I get to go visit her the day after school is out. Later the rest of the family come down and bring me home, but I like my private time better.

Getting to Aunt Harriett's is a forever drive from the Chicago suburbs where we live. The only nice thing about the trip is that we always have supper at a place that serves hot chocolate sundaes in huge, footed glasses. The scoop of ice cream, which is as big as a grapefruit, swims in thick chocolate sauce with a tower of whirled whipped cream and a cherry with a stem on top.

But the big difference isn't where other kids' relatives live but the way they are. Friends of mine, like Cassie and Jill, have grandmothers who do normal retired things like play golf and bridge and talk about arthritis. They go out to lunch a lot. They shop with their friends and then send their grandkids T-shirts with dolphins on them. They wear bright-colored clothes and a lot of jewelry and their faces are leathery from sun.

Aunt Harriett's face is wrinkled, but her skin

is very white. When she works outside, she wears a broad straw hat and gloves that turn back at the wrist. Instead of a little dog that will fit in a purse like Cassie's grandmother has, Aunt Harriett's dog, Rufus, is immense. Even though he smells like something dead most of the time, I really like him.

Aunt Harriett is very outspoken. (Mom calls it rude.) She hardly ever leaves home except to go to church. Her only real friend is a man named Aaron who lives there on the place and helps her. Jayne calls him an over-age hippie because he has a full beard and wears his hair in a ponytail. Actually he's a veteran and limps from an injury he got in Vietnam. I like Aaron because he doesn't talk any more than I do, and then only when he has something to say. He and Aunt Harriett are both into organic gardening and never kill anything.

Jayne is jealous. She thinks Aunt Harriett is partial to me because she goes to the trouble of picking out dolls for me, yet only sends Jayne money. Jayne started teasing me about getting dolls even before my friends did.

But I *did* like the movie Dad was sending me to again, and it would be fun to have the afternoon with Cassie. By the time I got dressed and went downstairs, I was humming the theme music to the movie, which I had memorized almost as well as I had the dialogue.

21

2
Clouded Windows

Cassie was already putting on one of her acts when she crawled into the front seat of Dad's car beside me. She chattered steadily in a voice that went up and down more than her natural one. Every time she finished a sentence she either smiled or twinkled at Dad and me by squinching up her eyes. I didn't say anything. I just sat there wishing she would be her real self instead of acting so affected in front of my dad. From the way he closed off his face to keep from showing his feelings, I knew he could hardly wait for us to get out of the car.

But she did look wonderful. She was wearing

her new white shorts with buckles on the cuffs, that pink scoop-necked T-shirt that makes her seem twice as tan as she really is, and too much cologne.

Oakbrook Center is only a few miles north of our village of Hinsdale, and we got there early. The mall is my favorite of all the ones I've ever seen. It not only has the fancy stores but it's pretty, with fountains and benches and growing flowers that are changed every season. The theater is across the street from the main part of the mall. I wanted to go over and window-shop but Cassie insisted that we wait in the movie lobby. I should have guessed right then that something was going on. Cassie sat very straight with her ankles crossed just so, as if she were posed for a picture. She kept looking around brightly and watching when new people came in the door.

The way she was showing off made me grumpier and grumpier until she finally got mad. "If you don't want to be here, go home," she said.

When I only shrugged and didn't answer, she sighed in a cross, heavy way. "Honestly, Emmy. I wonder if I can stand it until you grow up."

I stared at her. This was a girl who was exactly three months older than I. "Don't look at me like that," she said. "You know you're just sitting there sulking."

"I'm sitting here being honestly disgusted with you," I told her. "Nobody could be as happy and hyper as you're putting on."

"What a baby you are!" she said, tilting her chin up and looking away as if she didn't know me. "Either you don't say anything at all or you get nasty."

I didn't even look at her. It's my business if I don't want to chatter all the time, and, if I talk nasty, it's only because she drives me to it. The only people who never fuss at me about being too quiet are Dad and Aunt Harriett. One time, Maudie, Aunt Harriett's housekeeper, told Aunt Harriett that she thought the cat had gotten my tongue. Aunt Harriett only smiled and said she preferred the way I was to a lot of folks whose tongues were catty enough to feed a Feline Farm. I wasn't very old then and I had to look up "feline." Every once in a while, when Cassie starts in making fun of somebody's clothes or the way they act, I think about Aunt Harriett saying that and am glad that she hasn't ever met Cassie. I think Cassie might be hard to explain to Aunt Harriett.

I was still thinking about Aunt Harriett and what I would pack to take to her house on Friday when Cassie forgot about being cross at me and turned with that fake smile. "I know," she said brightly. "I'll get us both a Coke."

Before I could say anything, she was up and across the lobby, standing in line with other people who had come early and were buying things from the vendor. I watched her smile at the couple behind her and heard her laugh in a tinkly, artificial way as she got into some long conversation with them. Before she got back, the doors opened so that we could go inside.

The theater filled slowly. Just as the music started, a woman came groping her way down our row in the dark to take the seat beside Cassie. Cassie put her hand out and said quickly, "I'm really very sorry but this seat is taken."

When she felt my eyes on her, she whispered defensively, "Ben could come, you know."

That startled me enough that I didn't say anything. I like Cassie's brother, Ben. He's only a year ahead of us and probably the nicest guy in the eighth grade. He doesn't look a thing like Cassie, who is a brunette like her mother. Ben has Mr. Malone's coloring: hair that's blond, going on pink, and blue eyes. He looks a lot better than that sounds. Maybe the greatest thing about Ben is that becoming a teenager didn't ruin him. He's just as nice and easy going as he was when he was ten or twelve. He's gotten taller, of course, and his face either looks shaggy or sore, depending on whether he has tried to shave or not. Some days it looks pretty painful.

When the movie started, I leaned forward and hooked my arms over the empty seat in front of me. Every time I watch a movie I see something that I missed before. Sometimes I really have to concentrate to find anything I didn't notice the earlier times. Five minutes had passed or maybe ten when I heard a rustling and Cassie laughing softly.

I looked around, expecting to see Ben. Instead, Scott Lerner had settled into the seat Cassie had saved and already had his arm across the back of hers. He was looking down at her and smiling in that sneering way that he does. I turned away quickly.

I tried to get my head into the movie but I couldn't concentrate on it. As the story unfolded on the screen, I kept hearing Scott's whispered comments and Cassie's soft laughter of agreement. I don't like Scott Lerner. He wears his blond hair long and combed back high in a kind of pompadour that he pats carefully every once in a while. More than anything, he looks like a bleached Elvis Presley. Cassie has always told me she hated him because he was so completely stuck on himself and made fun of everybody who didn't agree with him about things. Yet here she was, making up to him in that bright, laughing kind of voice.

And what about Ben? What if Ben came in late and wanted that seat?

I punched Cassie.

When she looked around, I whispered, "Let's move."

She frowned, shook her head, and turned back to Scott.

The movie might as well have stopped as far as I was concerned. I stared at her. She couldn't have made arrangements to meet Scott in the movie! Or could she? My mind washed back over the whole afternoon, how dressed up she was, all that perfume, the way she had arched her back and looked at everyone who came in.

"Come to the restroom with me," I told her, punching her again.

She stared at me, ran her tongue lightly over her lips, and shook her head. When I asked her again, she tilted her chin that way she does and twisted around so that her whole back was turned to me.

I slid out of my seat and crept up the aisle. The light in the lobby seemed awfully bright after being inside. I didn't need to go to the restroom at all but I went in anyway. Maybe Cassie would change her mind and follow me. I washed my hands with that green soap that stings and held them under the blower until it gasped to a stop.

All right for Cassie, I thought. I would just plain go off and leave her. I had given her three chances to come with me. Who needed a friend that would let your dad pay for a movie ticket and set up a date with a worm like Scott Lerner on the sly? If Cassie Malone wanted to sit in there and make a fool of herself, she could just do it with Scott.

I really don't know how long it took me to walk home. Hinsdale is a long way from Oakbrook Center when you're not in a car. I remember I was tired by the time I got to York Road. I leaned against a fence and watched some couples wearing very bright clothes play golf. After that came the big sign announcing a polo game. I wished I could see the polo ponies from the road, but you never can. They had great pictures of them in the paper when Prince Philip of England came there to play. Everyone had expected him to fall off his horse, but he disappointed them.

By the time I reached Graue Mill, dusk was settling in. People were throwing bread chunks from a plastic bag to the mallards by the mill wheel. I sat cross-legged on a bench, wondering if the movie was over yet and what Cassie and Scott would do then.

Cassie wasn't going to get any sandwich at the French Baker because Dad had given the money to me.

Dad. Just thinking about Dad made a hard thump come in my stomach. What was he going to say about my leaving Cassie and walking all the way?

I slid off the bench and started to run.

The street lights came on when I was still a block from my house. Clouds of bugs circled the lamps, and fireflies winked here and there on peoples' lawns. Except when cars hummed by, the air throbbed around me with the rhythmic droning of insects. I ran past a house where the rich smoky smell of barbecued meat drowned out the scent of the flowers. I realized I was hungry.

When I turned our corner, I stopped. A big, long, fancy car was parked right in front of our house. I swallowed hard. The windows were all smoked out so you couldn't see in, but someone was sitting quietly in the front seat.

I stood a long time figuring out what to do. I wasn't about to go inside and interrupt whatever secret thing my dad had sent me away to keep from me. I didn't want to walk past that car with the man sitting in the front seat. I hesitated a minute, then cut back to the alley and went home that way. Murph heard me coming and began to bark and throw himself against his pen. I stopped and whispered him down to a happy whimper.

Whoever had been inside with Mom and Dad left. I heard the door of the car close and the faint hum of a motor pulling away. I was starting to go in to tell Mom and Dad I was home when the back door opened and they came out onto the redwood deck. Dad's words were indistinct but his tone was deep and solemn in a way that made my heart hurt.

Mom turned and leaned against him with her hands gripping his jacket lapels. Jacket? I'd never seen Dad wear a jacket at home on a Sunday evening before.

My mother's voice was almost a wail. "How can they blame us?" she asked miserably. "What do they think we can do about it? I don't know how to deal with this. I really don't."

Dad moved a chair and she sat down. He took the one beside her. I was in the shadows at the corner of the garage where the trumpet vine rears up and gropes in the air, its clusters of orange flowers pointed and curved like the fingers of witches. I couldn't move.

[If this had been a movie, they would have seen

me first. Dad would have leaped to his feet, probably knocking over the lawn chair with a great clat-
ter as he cried out into the darkness, "Who's there?"]

It wasn't a movie. Before either of them realized I was there, the kitchen phone rang. Mom rose
swiftly and went inside, her high heels chattering.
She flicked on the light and I heard her ask in a
rising tone, "Emmy? Why, I don't know."

I knew that had to be Cassie's mother calling.
I knew that it was too late ever to explain why I
went off and left Cassie, or why I had been standing in the shadows without letting them know I
was there. I also knew that the quicker they found
out I was safe at home and all right, the better it
would be.

When I stepped into the light falling from the
kitchen window, Dad looked at me, first startled,
then angry. He didn't ask where I had come from
or where I had been or anything. He only barked
at me in his grown-up voice and asked, "How long
have you been standing there listening?"

Then Mom came to the door. She glanced at
me, went back to the phone, and then came back
out.

"Well, young lady?" she said, in that tone she
uses when I'm in trouble. "It looks as if you have
some explaining to do."

Why hadn't I used all that time walking home

to figure out what I was going to tell them? I couldn't come right out and say that Cassie had sneaked a date with Scott Lerner and it made me mad. Never mind how fed up I get at Cassie and how sick I get of her play-acting. She's my friend. I shook my head.

"I wanted to come home," I said flatly.

My father trembled with anger. His words came clipped and pushing. "That's all, Emmy?"

I nodded.

He rose, muttered something under his breath, and stamped off into the darkness of the back yard.

"Bed," Mom said, looking at me in an angry, level way. "No book, no stereo, no TV, just bed."

At the kitchen door, I looked back.

She turned, crossed her arms against her chest as if she were hugging herself, and followed my father off into the darkness.

3
Sudden Silences

That Monday was the last day I would ever be twelve in my life and I woke up with a knot instead of food in my stomach. I had gone to bed as Mom told me to. I had even gone to sleep, probably because I'm not used to taking long walks like that. I didn't really wake up when Jayne came in, but I did hear Geoff's car pull away from the curb with a squeal.

I hated getting up because I knew the business about walking home from Oakbrook wasn't over. Mom and Dad would talk to me, this time in a carefully light, understanding tone because they weren't afraid or mad any more. They would ask me why I had done such a stupid thing as walk out of a movie and leave my friend there and worry everybody half to death. I still didn't know what to tell them that wouldn't cause them to dislike Cassie even more than they already did.

A red cardinal rocked back and forth, singing, on a branch outside while I pulled up the covers on my bed. I stood in the window and listened carefully. He sang, *"Wheet, wheet, cheedle, chew, pink,"* then hopped to another branch and sang it again. Aunt Harriett has cardinals at her place in Missouri, too, and they sing like rollicking thunder. She can always tell them apart by their songs. I wrote, *"Wheet, wheet, cheedle, chew, pink,"* on a memo sheet and pinned it to my bulletin board. That way I would recognize that bird the next time he came, the same way Aunt Harriett always recognizes her birds. Sometimes she gives her cardinals names, and she always puts out food for them in winter. They come back because she says they never range any farther than nine miles from where they were hatched.

When I couldn't put it off any longer, I hugged my books tight against my chest and went downstairs. I deliberately didn't look at Aunt Harriett's package in the hall. It *couldn't* be a doll. I just had to keep telling myself that. As much as I disliked the idea of being a teenager, I had to grow up sometime. Grownups don't get dolls.

It was so quiet in the kitchen that I thought everyone had left. Instead, Mom and Dad were in the breakfast room with Jayne. When I came in, Dad was leaning toward Jayne and talking in a low, earnest tone. He glanced up, straightened, and fell silent when he saw me.

"There she is, our Emmy," Mom said brightly, getting up in a little rush. She poured me a glass of orange juice and stuck a bran muffin into the microwave oven to warm for me.

Dad picked up the folded newspaper from beside his plate, but his eyes were on Jayne. She got up without looking at him and set her cereal bowl in the sink. Jayne is five years older than I am and a lot prettier than I would ever admit to her. She looks just the way a senior in high school graduating with honors should look. Or maybe like a freshman at Northwestern, since that is where she had been accepted for the coming fall.

Jayne's hair is dark and falls loose, the way hair does in shampoo ads on TV. Her eyes are a very dark brown like Mom's, and her face is too small for her eyes, which makes her resemble a kitten. That morning her eyes looked dull, without the little points of light that usually shine out under her lashes.

I wanted to scream, "What's going on here?" Instead, I put butter on my muffin and watched it run in a golden stream around the raisins that humped up on the top. My stomach felt tight, waiting for the lecture I knew was coming.

Instead, Dad put the still-folded *Chicago Tribune* by his plate and left without a word. Mom glanced at me and followed him. Right then I decided that whatever was going on had something to do with Jayne. I had never seen her look that miserable in my whole life.

I stared at the muffin. The raisins were staring back at me like eyes. The melted butter didn't look golden any more but just greasy. I stuffed the muffin in the garbage disposal, poured my orange juice down after it, and left for school.

Cassie walked around all day with Scott Lerner and wouldn't even look at me. I wanted to explain why I'd left, but she didn't give me a chance. I wanted to be angry at her, but instead I hurt inside my chest.

Then I went home from school and found a note from Mom saying that she and Dad and Jayne would all be out. Derek was going to sit for me and I wasn't to give him any trouble.

Derek is sixteen and disgusting. He heated a pan of lasagna and put it on the table without placemats or anything. When I served myself, he didn't even glance at me but just went on stuffing himself. He ate with both arms on the table while he read a copy of *Car and Driver*.

"Quit staring at me with that blank face," he ordered. "Eat your dinner."

The lasagna tasted like cardboard. "What's going on?" I asked him. "Who was here in that big car last night? Why are Dad and Jayne acting so strange?"

"Eat or leave the table," he said, without looking up.

"I want to know what's going on," I practically yelled.

He looked up at me then, with his eyes flat and hostile. "You have finals tomorrow. Go upstairs and study."

"I don't have to," I told him, glaring.

He wagged his head toward Mom's note on the refrigerator. "Read my lips," he said acidly, then soundlessly mouthed, "Don't give Derek any trouble."

"I hate you," I told him.

He laughed with his mouth full. "Listen to my heart break."

Up in my room, I lay in the dark wishing I could run away somewhere, maybe to Aunt Harriett's, so I wouldn't have to go through the rest of the week.

I thought about Jayne and how strange and sad she had seemed that morning. A terrible loneliness for the old Jayne swept over me. Once when she and I had been sharing the blue room at Aunt Harriett's, a storm blew up. The shutters had chattered at the windows, and we heard a sound as if somebody were dragging one foot across the floor of the room upstairs.

"What's that?" Jayne whispered from the other bed. Her tone was cross but her voice quivered as if she were afraid.

Before I could even answer, Aunt Harriett had appeared at our door. She was wearing a long dark robe, and her hair was pulled back in a fat braid with curls springing out of its end. She was smiling.

"Don't fret about that noise," she told us. "Old houses talk to themselves, just the way old people do. That's only the poor captain. He came back here to live after he lost a leg in the Spanish American War, you know. They tell me he hated windy nights, so he paces around, dragging that peg along." She smiled at us and disappeared into the darkness.

That was when Jayne jumped out of her bed and came over to get in bed with me. "Emmy," she whispered. "Don't tell me she really believes in ghosts!"

"Not the way you mean," I said. It was hard to explain then, and it still is. I tried to tell Jayne how the people Aunt Harriett had heard about and lived with in that house were still so alive in her mind that she liked thinking of them there with her.

"Well, *I* don't like it," Jayne said crossly, not moving to go back to her own bed. I wanted to giggle then, but I didn't.

Jayne and I used to giggle together a lot. I *really* wanted Jayne back the way she used to be, but I would have settled for the way she had been since becoming a teenager. Even a sister who was conceited and cross was better than one who looked so miserable that she made a hard lump come in my throat.

Our house was anything but silent. I listened to its noises. Downstairs the dishwasher pumped, washing up the dishes Derek and I had used at dinner. Derek's radio pulsed the beat of his favorite rock group, and the air conditioner came on and off.

I hated living in a house whose only ghosts were those of engineers!

Then I made a list in my head of all the hateful things about my life.

I hated having my stomach hurt and not being able to get food to go down because of something about Jayne that everybody was keeping from me.

I hated having a birthday that turned me thirteen when I can count on the fingers of one hand the number of teenagers I really like.

I hated leaving the seventh grade and having to start all over again in the eighth.

Most of all, I hated the thought of going through that whole last week of school alone. I wouldn't have anyone to walk around with after finals. I would end up by myself at the All School Frolic on Thursday. The final assembly would be the worst. I'd have to stand up with everyone staring at me and not a single person to clap especially for me.

I felt bad about whatever was making Jayne so miserable, but I cried about Cassie.

4
Black Tuesday

I've always had this theory that parents never really *see* you. Instead, they just look to see what needs to be done to you. By the morning of my birthday, I was absolutely convinced that neither of my parents was even conscious that I was still alive. Whatever was at the bottom of their whispered conversations and their unexplained absences and the sick, fearful way they looked at Jayne had shoved me right out of their minds.

Therefore I was astonished when Mom wished me "Happy Birthday" and gave me one of those inspecting glances. "What's wrong, Emmy?" she asked.

I just shook my head, thinking I should be asking *her*.

"Emmy," she said, letting her voice turn spiky and irritated. "Haven't I got enough on my mind with Jayne"—she paused, flushed, and finished in a milder tone—"with Jayne's graduation? I certainly don't need to have you marching around here with that long face on your own birthday. Tell us what's wrong and we'll try to fix it."

"It's not anything that anybody can fix," I replied.

"Give us a try," Dad said, pulling himself out of the *Tribune* to look over at me.

What was I going to tell them? That I was sick of being treated like a stranger in my own house? That I was tired of being chattered at and patronized and wanted to be a human being, too?

"Okay," I said, cross at myself for being a chicken. "I don't feel like having a birthday. I just plain don't want to turn thirteen."

I don't know what I expected, but it wasn't for Dad to give Mom one of those indulgent looks and laugh for the first time in a week.

Mom didn't laugh. "That's poppycock," she said

sharply. Then she frowned and stared at me as if she were really trying to figure out where I was coming from. But she's a practical person. Her mind can stretch only so far before it jerks back like an elastic band and takes its original shape. Fact is always fact to Mom. "There's no place to go after twelve except thirteen," she reminded me. I sighed at how hopeless this whole conversation was. Did she and Dad really think that children live in some airy, fairy place where everything is nicer than it will ever be again? Just because we're smaller doesn't mean our problems don't fill our slightly smaller lives as completely as theirs do!

They both waited for me to say something they could respond to. I chickened out again and decided to keep myself to myself. But first I had to deal with what I *had* told them. Since it was so great to hear Dad laugh, I thought I might try for that again. It helps that grownups have trouble thinking and laughing at the same time. I produced a reasonable facsimile of a smile and said, "Come on, you all! Admit twelve is better! It doesn't repeat itself like eleven. Chocolate-covered marshmallow Easter eggs come in boxes of twelve. With a box of twelve crayons, you can color anything in the world."

Both of them relaxed visibly. Then, because Mom is so practical, she had to add, "But just think! You'll officially be a teenager."

Didn't she realize that was the problem, not a solution? And how could I tell two people who already had two teenagers in Jayne and Derek that I just plain didn't like teenagers and didn't want to join the club?

I don't just *think* thirteen is an unlucky number, I know it is. Jane spelled her name sensibly until that fatal birthday. Then it got that silly *y* in the middle. She also got crosser for no reason, and started mucking up her face and dying her hair and hanging around with weird people like that Geoff Wheaton.

Derek wasn't any better. I can remember when he was real. He taught me to tie my shoes and throw a ball underhanded. Then, on his thirteenth birthday, he was completely transformed into a pure plastic prototype. He started laughing at things he didn't think were funny and speaking entirely in slogans as if he were on television.

And look at Cassie, if you could stand to.

Both Mom and Dad had slipped away again. They looked at each other the strange, intense way they had since Sunday, and after a minute Dad caught himself and reached over to pat my hand.

"You're right, Emmy. But there's nothing we can do about your turning thirteen except enjoy it." He rose and leaned to kiss me. "Happy Birthday, Kitten. See you tonight."

I got all through my morning classes without having to look at either Cassie or Scott Lerner. My luck ran out at noon. Cassie came into the cafeteria alone and brought her tray over to sit down at our regular table. Jill was already there with her best friend, Mandy.

Maybe I'm kidding myself but, in my heart, I still don't think Cassie started out to be mean. It's just that she was completely giddy with having a boyfriend. When she realized that she had a built-in audience at our table, with a bunch of boys also sitting close enough to hear, she couldn't resist putting on one of her show-off acts.

"I can tell you what Emmy is getting for her thirteenth birthday," she announced to everyone at the table, her dark eyes sparkling.

"You wouldn't tell!" Jill said, horrified.

Cassie laughed. "Emmy knows. She always knows. Every year, no matter how old she gets, her Aunt Harriett sends her a doll. Can't you just see her, grown up and in high school—maybe even married with kids—and still getting a doll every birthday? When I turned thirteen, I got a new stereo," she added smugly.

"Is that true?" Jill asked me, ignoring the bragging part about the stereo. "Will you really get a doll?"

"They're not just regular dolls," I told her, feeling the red crawl up my neck so my freckles stood out. When Cassie made a funny little jeering sound, I glared at her. "Lots of grown-up people collect dolls."

Cassie laughed. "Like your Aunt Harriett back in that hick town in Missouri?"

I had already told Jill and Mandy about the good times I have when I'm back in Missouri with Aunt Harriett. Jill either remembered or just didn't like Cassie's tone any better than I did. She challenged her. "Have you ever been there?" she asked.

"I don't have to go there to know I hate it," Cassie said. "I wouldn't live in a place like that if you paid me. When I grow up, I'm going to live in Beverly Hills."

"And be a movie star, I guess," Jill said, standing up with her tray and turning her back on Cassie. Then she smiled down at me. "Have a happy birthday, Emmy, doll or no doll!" (You can probably tell from this that Jill hadn't had that fatal birthday yet.)

"I *am* going to be a movie star," Cassie called after her. "I really am."

I felt my face getting red from the way everybody was looking around and tittering. If only Cassie wouldn't always make a big scene. "Come on, Cassie," I whispered. "Jill didn't mean anything by that."

"I know what she meant," Cassie said. "You know it, too. You believe me, don't you? Haven't I always planned to be a movie star as long as you can remember?

"First I'm going to be a model," she went on angrily. "Then they'll ask me to do commercials on TV and, after that, movies. Then, when I am rich and famous, I'll write a book about my experiences and be interviewed on talk shows."

She looked at me sideways to see what I was thinking. I didn't say anything, but she lashed out at me again anyway.

"See, there you go, Emmy, not saying anything, just thinking that I can't do it. How is a person supposed to become a success when even her best friend doesn't believe in her?"

"You can't read my mind," I told her.

"I can see through you just as if you didn't have a face," Cassie said. "You're thinking that I'm short and models are always tall. You're thinking

47

I'm not pretty enough and don't know how to act." Her voice kept getting higher and louder until some older kids who were walking by turned around to stare at us.

If there's one thing I hate about myself the very worst, it's the way I blush. Even though it was Cassie who was making the scene, I blushed and kept on getting hotter and redder until my face felt swollen.

"Cassie," I said carefully, knowing the rest of the kids in the cafeteria could hear every word we said. "Be quiet or I'm going to get up and walk away."

Cassie leaped to her feet. "*You're* going to walk away? Didn't you learn anything doing it the last time?" With that she grabbed her books and flounced out the door.

I got up without looking at anyone, wishing I could sink right through the floor. I was almost to the waste bin when somebody gripped the edge of my tray. I looked up to see Cassie's brother, Ben, holding it and grinning at me. "Good riddance," he said, smiling. "Forget Mammoth Mouth and have a happy birthday. What do you want, anyway?"

"I'm easy to please," I told him.

I must have told Ben the truth, because that few minutes with him made me feel cheery the rest of the afternoon. I didn't even mind having to walk home alone because Cassie was off with Scott. The Russian olive trees along the parkway were in bloom. Their tiny, spiky yellow flowers looked as if they had been pinched from wax, and they smelled like spice when I pulled them close. I didn't pick any because each one of them will make a little hard olive, given time.

But Cassie, with her scene about the doll, had still managed to make me dread opening my present from Aunt Harriett.

I passed the table in the hall without looking at that present and went up to my room. I found an old Rosalind Russell movie on TV and watched it until Mom called me to come down and set the table. Only then did Mom think to ask if Cassie was coming. I shook my head and went back off into the dining room so she couldn't ask me why.

When I sat down at the table, I realized that my birthday dinner was the first meal I had eaten with Jayne since Sunday. She didn't seem to be very hungry, and she looked pale even under her blusher. She passed the food, but was careful not to look at Dad, who kept watching her with an expression of concern.

My haunting sense of dread got worse when

Mom brought out the packages. Dad looked curiously at Aunt Harriett's box. "What kind of a doll do you suppose it is this time?" he asked, glancing over at Mom as he spoke.

Mom shrugged. "I'm sure it's very special," she said. "Open it, Emmy. We're all waiting."

Something funny happened in my chest. I've been called Emmy all my life, but suddenly it annoyed me. I felt cross at Mom, for hardly any reason at all. But my name *is* Emily. Why had they gone to the trouble of giving me a perfectly suitable grown-up name if they weren't ever going to use it?

Under the balloon gift wrap, the box was plain brown with no printing on it, and the tissue paper was a soft cocoa color instead of white. I lifted the tissue and looked into the box. With my first glance, the cold shiver came back. Without even thinking, I covered the doll's head again very quickly with the paper.

I felt funny and scared and my heart began banging hard, the way it used to when I was at Aunt Harriett's and I'd hear her piano in the middle of the night, even though I knew there was no living person downstairs.

5
The Sunday Doll

I could feel my family watching me, Jayne with
her intent brown eyes under black lashes that curved
up to touch the skin above her eyelids. Jayne's lashes
don't naturally curve like that. She brushes them
with mascara and then bends them with a curler.
Derek was smiling that half smile that's almost the
same as a sneer. Mom and Dad just looked curious
and waited.

Even through the paper, I could still see the
doll. It had imprinted its image into my memory
in that split second. Its dress was made of dark green
cotton with a full skirt that almost reached the an-

kles. The dress was covered by a straight dark apron that hung from the shoulders and was only a little bit shorter than the dress. The shoes were sturdy and black, with the toes pointing up at me out of the folded tissue paper.

The doll had straight brown hair like mine, only longer. You couldn't see much of its hair, which had been twisted back underneath a really darling black bonnet with a stiff brim.

But the doll had no face, only a pale, flesh-colored expanse where its eyes and nose and mouth should have been.

"What's wrong, Emmy?" Dad asked, with just a hint of impatience.

"It's different," I said, handing the box over to him.

"Of course it's different," he replied indulgently. "Aunt Harriett picks out dolls too carefully to duplicate what you already have." As he spoke, he turned back the paper. Even Jayne, who had sat listlessly, hardly touching her dinner, craned with Mom to look into the box.

"Oh, Emmy," Mom breathed. "It's an Amish doll. How beautiful!"

Jayne leaned back in her chair. "Aunt Harriett really knows you, Emmy! That doll has the exact same expression you always have."

"Jayne!" Mom cried, turning with a look of astonishment. "What a thing to say! The doll is beautiful, but our Emmy's face is anything but blank."

That made Derek curious enough to stand up and peer over into the box. "Jayne's on the button, Mom. That's the look Emmy gets on her face every time you try to tell her anything."

"That's enough of that," Mom said sharply, without contradicting him.

Suddenly I could hear Cassie's voice as clearly as if she were in the room: "I can see through you just as if you didn't have a face."

Dad was studying me, his eyes troubled. "You looked as if the doll scared you."

I shrugged. "I don't know why I did. I know it's only a doll, but. . ."

"It *is* spooky," he said, his tone thoughtful as Mom lifted the doll out of the box. "Why do you suppose they don't finish them, put on the face and all?" he asked her.

Mom held the doll in one hand and smoothed its apron with the other. As she did, I saw a glint of white petticoat in under its long skirt. "Because of some quotation from the Bible," she said. "The one that forbids making graven images."

From the back, the doll looked charming, with

its full wide skirt and sturdy legs in real knitted socks. But more than anything, I didn't want Mom to turn that eyeless face to me again. "It is beautiful," she said. "So different from anything you have. What in the world will you ever name it?"

I said the name without even thinking of it first. "The Sunday Doll," I said. Then, because everybody looked at me, I tried to explain. "Well, it came on Sunday, and, because of the Bible verse and all . . ." I let my voice trail off. I didn't want to add what I was thinking—that, even if I were still playing with dolls, I would never play with this one. Not and have that bleak, blank face staring back at me.

Inside, I was ruffled with resentment. I wanted to tell them all that if I looked as blank in the face as the doll did, I at least had my reasons. It was the only way to deal with a family that shut you out, treated you like a child, and thought they could talk you into anything.

"The Sunday Doll," Dad repeated aloud to himself. "I like that, I really do." Then he stretched and pulled a slim package from his back pocket and smiled at me "Happy Birthday, Kitten." I opened the box and let him fasten a wonderful new watch on my arm. The plastic case was bright pink, big and round with a second hand and an alarm, and the date showing through a little window.

"Maybe you'll have better luck with this one," he told me, patting my wrist and smiling. For once he didn't go on and tease me about sowing the world with lost watches the way Johnny Appleseed had with apple cores.

Mom's box held the sweater she and I had looked at together. Instead of the apricot color I liked and a size extra large, which was what I wanted because my figure is getting so bumpy, the sweater was that same deep blue she always buys me and in a size medium.

Jayne gave me bath oil that smelled like roses, and Derek's box, which was almost too heavy to lift, held a set of five-pound weights. "Everybody's into fitness," he said defensively, obviously a little embarrassed by Dad's startled look. "See, they have Velcro so you can tape them on when you exercise."

The cake was chocolate with green mint filling and white frosting. I put the lid back on the doll box while Dad was lighting the candles. *Thirteen* candles.

Just knowing that doll was in there, its blank face pressed against the brownish paper, raised the hair along my arms. I never meant to open that box again in my whole entire life. I would simply write Aunt Harriett a thank-you note, hide the doll on my closet shelf, and try to forget I had ever seen it.

Because it was my birthday, I didn't have to help with dishes. I offered to anyway, because Dad took Jayne off into the study and shut the door. When Mom shook her head, I cut myself another piece of cake to take in by the TV. She saw me put the cake on a napkin and turned. "I'm sorry Cassie couldn't make it tonight. If you want to take some cake to her and Ben, there are plastic plates in that cupboard."

I thanked her, but I didn't cut any cake for Cassie or Ben. Maybe the way the doll affected me was partly Cassie's fault. Maybe I would have liked it fine if she hadn't made that big public scene about it before I even saw it.

I wrote Aunt Harriett three thank-you notes before I thought one sounded right. I put the envelope on the hall table for Dad to send out. Even though I would be there myself on Friday, Aunt Harriett loves to get mail.

When it was my bedtime, I turned off the TV and carried my presents upstairs. I put the perfumed oil in the bathroom I share with the other kids, left the five-pound weights out on my desk where Derek could find them without rummaging through my stuff, and tried on the sweater.

I was right. Medium was too small. It was long enough and the sleeves came down to cover my wrists, but my chest stuck out in it too much to wear it to school.

That only left the doll for me to deal with.

Who ever heard of a doll without a face, anyway?

I looked along my shelf of dolls and saw their faces a new way. The first two, and the most worn, were baby dolls with curved legs and dimples and little short wisps of hair, always brown like mine. After that, Aunt Harriett had gone to toddler dolls. These dolls all were still chubby and had fatter faces than I've ever had, but they were children, not babies. The last six were all character dolls dressed in wonderfully complete outfits—a ballerina all in pink who never could get off her toes, a Red Riding Hood whose basket I had managed to lose, and some characters from favorite stories of mine.

It was funny how seeing a doll without a face made all the rest of them look a little too smiling and silly. Their cheeks were too pink and their lashes looked fakey, like Jayne's. Even though there was plenty of room on the shelf, I put the box with the Sunday Doll way to the back on my closet shelf and went to bed with the alarm on my pink watch set for seven in the morning.

I don't know how long I had been asleep when something wakened me. I sat straight up, scared for no reason. The first thing I thought of was that faceless doll, staring without eyes into its tissue paper. After just a moment, I realized what had really wakened me. Jayne had gotten a phone of her own on her sixteenth birthday, after she promised to pay the monthly bills from her allowance and babysitting money. I had been awakened by the sound of that phone ringing softly in the next room.

According to my new pink watch, it was almost one o'clock, which seemed awfully late to get a call. I couldn't hear what Jayne was saying but she was whispering urgently, her voice rising and falling the way it does when she is trying to talk you into something.

Finally I heard her say, "Please, Geoff, please," in a very breathless way, and then it was silent. *Geoff*. It took me a long time to go back to sleep again, because I kept thinking I could hear her crying behind the plaster and years that separated us.

6
Ben Malone

The last thing I expected that next morning was for Cassie to call me to wait up and walk to school with her. But I waited, hating myself for being such a pushover to make up with. As I watched her walk toward me, I had a funny sense of unreality, as if neither of us were the people we really were. She didn't even look like herself. Instead of jeans and a shirt, she was wearing a blue cotton skirt with sandals, and her hair was pulled back with a ribbon. When she got close to me, I could see blue smudges on her eyelids. and little stiff droplets of mascara on her lashes, which was silly because her eyelashes are already naturally black. I felt a little surge of anger in the back of my throat. One word about the doll and she was going to get it.

But she didn't say anything at all about the doll. She acted as if I hadn't gone off and left her at the movie house or had that fight with her in the cafeteria. She just fell into step and started talking about the tryouts. It took me a minute to remember that the Park and Recreation Department had scheduled tryouts for a summer music program the night before. "I would have called you to go with me," she said. "Then I remembered it was your birthday, and anyway a friend asked me and I just went."

I felt her watching me. "Oh, I meant to tell you," she went on. "I ordered something wonderful for your birthday but it hasn't come."

I nodded, knowing that wasn't the truth but not really caring. My silence was awkward enough to make her cross. "I hate that babyish way you clam up and don't say anything," she told me. "You don't even care what I ordered for you. You don't even care who asked me to go out last night."

It was mean of me but, since I really *didn't* care, I halfway changed the subject. "How were the tryouts?" I asked.

"Hilarious!" she said swiftly. "Absolutely the

funniest thing you ever saw in your whole life. One town clown after another."

I did look at her then. "Comedy routines? I thought it was going to be all music."

She shook her head, smiling as if someone had trained a camera on her. "No, *they* were serious! All those kids up there sweating away, making dreadful noises and thinking they were musicians."

I felt rude words piling up behind my tongue. What had she thought she was going to hear, the Chicago Symphony? But I didn't say anything. I just started walking faster so this would be over quicker.

She took little swift steps to keep up with me. "And I wish you could have seen Megan Abbot up there sawing away on her violin with her chin stuck out like a bulldog," she went on. "You would have died laughing."

"I would not," I said flatly.

Cassie stopped and stared at me with those eyes that look like melted chocolate. "What's that about?" she asked.

I kept on walking, even though my stomach always flutters when Cassie challenges me straight on like that.

"I would not have died laughing," I told her. "I wouldn't have laughed at all. It's not funny when somebody does the best she can. Megan can't help it if you're jealous because she can play the violin and you can't."

"I wouldn't play the violin if you paid me," Cassie said angrily. "I just said she looked stupid and she did. Anyway, who are you to say how she looked when you weren't even there?"

I forced myself to look her right in the eye. "I'm Emily Prentice. I have a perfect right to tell you I hate hearing you cut everybody down with your mouth."

She looked stunned, then jerked her head as if she were a puppet on a string. "Listen to Miss Prentice," she mocked me. "I'm not cutting everybody down. I was only telling you about last night, and you started getting nasty."

"You weren't telling me about the tryouts," I told her. "You were making fun of every single person who had the nerve to get up there on that stage. I guess you think it makes you better than they are when you cut them down like that."

When Cassie gets mad her face swells and you see white all the way around her eyes. "A lot of nerve you have, Emmy Prentice," she shouted at me. "If you don't think it was a freak show, ask Scott Lerner. I was with him, and he thought it was as funny as I did."

There. She had been dying to tell me that it was Scott Lerner who had asked her. If I hadn't already guessed it when she told me about going, I would have known from the way she was talking. Scott is one of those boys who sits in the back of a classroom and makes fun of everyone's answers. And that's exactly what Cassie had sounded like, a female impersonation of Scott Lerner without an Elvis Presley pompadour.

I would have told her that, too, except that she strode away as fast as anyone can in those sandals with the backs out that look more like bedroom slippers than shoes, anyway. Her nose was really up in the air and her shoulders moved more than they needed to.

I stood looking after her with my stomach fluttering. I could take Cassie's scenes, even her showing off. But when people cut other people down and laugh, I really can't stand it.

Was it possible for a friendship to end like this, all those years disappearing in a few minutes?

"Happy Birthday, Emily," I whispered out loud.

"Talking to yourself?" a voice behind me asked.

I turned, blushing, and saw Ben standing there, grinning at me. "Meet your destiny, Emmy Prentice," he said solemnly. "Life for you is one Malone after another. Every time my sister stamps off mad, I appear as if by magic, filling the empty slot."

I laughed. "You could tell she was mad, then."

He nodded seriously. "She is an interesting study, that girl. She has given up the entire middle range of emotions. She now either tweets and burbles with happiness or blazes with rage. All the world's a stage, and Cassie is out to star in every role."

"Thirteen," I told him.

"Is that a signal for something?"

I shrugged. "Haven't you noticed how people turn weird when they turn thirteen?"

"You look pretty normal—nice and normal, in fact," he said, and I could feel him really looking at me as he said it.

Why did I have to blush? He didn't mean anything by that. He only meant I wasn't making a scene. "Give me time," I told him. "It'll probably hit me, too."

"Now that," he said soberly, "is what I call threatening news." His tone turned very casual. "Say, while you're still fun to be around, want to go to the all school bash with me Thursday? That way I can enjoy your company before you turn weird, as you put it."

I stared at him. All school bash. He must mean

the All School Frolic. The Parents Club throws it every year, the day before school is out. Cassie and I had talked about going together. We had even decided what we would wear.

Ben did a little accurate mind reading. "If you're thinking about Cass, she's going with Scott Lerner. Breakfast this morning was the scene of a lively performance. Cass regaled us all with grand hysterics. The upshot was that she was going to die— 'literally die' was her phrase—if she didn't get to buy a new outfit before the sun sets tonight."

"To cook hot dogs and play softball in?" I asked, without thinking.

"You got it!" He nodded. "But clearly she's either going to be dead or prancing around with Scott Lerner, which leaves you free. Are you game to go with me?"

Instant scrambled brains. What should I do? Those All School Frolics literally last forever. The idea of trailing around by myself the livelong day was horrifying. And I liked Ben. But I had never thought of myself as a girl who would walk around all day with a boy, even someone's brother.

Maybe my brains really were scrambled, because I felt myself nodding. "I'd like that," I told him. "I really would."

He grinned in a way that made me want to

grin back. Then he reached out and touched the face of my watch with a single finger. "Better check and see if this sharp new pink timepiece is guaranteed safe underwater."

I did laugh then. At the picnic the year before, some kids got hold of the hose that was plugged into the hydrant in case the charcoal burners got out of hand. I wasn't the only one who'd gone home looking like a drowned rat.

We went up the school steps together. Ben held the door for me and then took off. But he waved at me as he tore down the hall toward his homeroom.

Cassie sat with Scott Lerner at lunch, and Jill was the only person besides Ben who mentioned my new watch all day.

After I got through my final tests, I cleaned out my locker into a plastic bag Mom had sent with me because she knows all about the end of school.

Cassie didn't even show up at her locker, which is right next to mine. I was glad and sorry, both at the same time, and decided not to try to figure out why.

Dinner was strange. Derek was off with his gang at a pizza party, and Jayne had a headache and didn't come to the table. Mom took her a tray with some of the barbecued brisket left over from my birthday dinner and a little salad. I'm always quiet at dinner, but that night Mom and Dad were, too. Dad said something about the weather and Mom nodded absently. After it got too quiet, Mom looked startled and tried something about the news. When that didn't work any better, they both fell silent. The only thing I could think of to mention was that Ben Malone had asked me to go to the All School Frolic, but I was embarrassed to bring it up.

As I got up to clear the table, Dad smiled at me. "We didn't even ask how your day was, Kitten."

I shrugged. "Okay, I guess," I told him. "I cleaned out my locker."

Mom groaned, and Dad laughed because he knows about the end of school, too.

Ben Malone called a little after seven. Mom answered the phone and handed it to me, frankly curious about who it was. I flushed because I can't stand it when people make a big deal out of things. I covered the phone with my hand and whispered to her that it was Cassie's brother. She nodded and was turning away when I had to speak to her again.

"Ben thinks we should bike down to Jaspar's for a sundae to celebrate finishing our finals," I told her.

Mom nodded. "Good idea! Just don't be late."

I went upstairs to wash my hands and comb my hair. For some reason the light in the bathroom seemed more glaring than usual so that my face really stared back at me.

I look at other people so much I forget that I don't look like them. How could I have brown eyes like Jayne's and hair almost as dark as Cassie's and still look like nothing at all? The Sunday Doll in the living flesh, I told myself bitterly. The features were there, but so lightly etched that they might as well have been flat muslin like the doll's.

I frowned, wondering if my eyes would look better if I drew black lines around them. And maybe a touch of blusher would make my skin appear to have blood under it.

I had Jayne's make-up kit unzipped before I regained my sanity. What was the matter with me? I'd been thirteen only one day and already I was thinking about mucking up my face!

I toweled my cheeks hard, which made them plenty pink enough, and ran downstairs to get my bike.

7

Guilt on Guilt

The concrete benches outside Jaspar's are set under a row of cottonwood trees. Those benches are always cold and feel filthy because of crusty stuff that drops out of the trees. But the hedges that separate that benched area from the street smell wonderful.

Ben is fun to listen to. When he tells a story, he uses words you don't expect. When he comes to the end, he looks at you intently, his pale eyelashes startling next to the vivid blue of his eyes. He doesn't laugh until you do, and then it's more like a chuckle.

I felt comfortable being there with him. I liked it until I realized that probably Mom thought Cassie was with us, too. Then I started feeling guilty, even though I hadn't done anything wrong at all. Right about then the next horrible thought struck me. What if Ben thought this was a date? What if he thought I liked him well enough that he could try to kiss me or something? After that I wasn't comfortable with Ben at all.

In fact, I just kept waiting for him to take me home and leave.

As we skidded to a stop in my driveway, the same long dark car that had been leaving the night I walked home from the movie pulled away from the curb. Ben looked after it and whistled.

"Boy, that Geoff Wheaton is one lucky pup. Fat chance my dad would let me drive a boat like that if he had one."

I stared after the car. Because of the black windows I hadn't seen the driver and I couldn't imagine that Ben had. Anyway, Geoff usually drove a little red car with flame stripes down the side and a plastic red devil fastened to the radio aerial.

"Was that Geoff?" I asked.

He shrugged. "That's the Wheaton car. There aren't that many cars like that around here. And who else would have driven it over here to your house?"

Suddenly I was more confused than ever. If that *was* the Wheaton car, what had it been doing at our house on Sunday? Geoff hadn't been driving it then, because he and Jayne were out together. I retraced that day in my mind. Mom had taken a phone call that upset her. So Dad had shipped me off with Cassie—because the Wheatons were coming over? But why?

Ben's mind was still on the Wheatons, too. "Of course, there aren't too many families around here who live like the Wheatons do."

"How do you know so much about Geoff's family?" I asked.

He looked at me. "You know Seth, the short blond kid I hang around with?" I nodded. "Seth's mom and dad both work for the Wheatons, and they live in a little apartment over the garage. I've never gone there with him, but Seth says that place is a layout—stables, tennis courts, an army of servants."

"Army, Ben?" I asked, grinning at him.

He laughed. "Okay, maybe just a platoon. Besides Seth's dad, there's a man who tends the horses, and that guy who drives the car. I think Seth's mom just cooks, but she may clean house, too. Can you picture Geoff's mother whipping around that place with a dust mop and a vacuum sweeper?"

Then he looked at me and grinned. "Don't misunderstand me. I wouldn't trade places with Geoff for anything. I couldn't make it in a pressure cooker. And to quote a little Dickens, Geoff's family is into Great Expectations."

When I looked puzzled, he shrugged. "His dad had his heart set on Geoff's going to his old Ivy League school back East. When Geoff didn't make it on grades, his dad practically threatened to sue the school."

"Come on, Ben," I said. He was sounding like Cassie.

"Okay, maybe I'm exaggerating, but, according to Seth, Mr. Wheaton has been kicking up a real fuss. He wanted the school to give Geoff the tests again. He even threatened to send Geoff off for some remedial brains to get him accepted by fall."

I stared at Ben, remembering Jayne's pleading voice repeating Geoff's name in the middle of the night.

"That's ugly," I said. "What's so big about the East? Chicago's got a lot of colleges. For instance, there's Northwestern. That's where Jayne's going."

He smiled. "It takes a whale of a test score to get in there, too. But what's all that to us? We have *years* before we have to bite our pencils through the SATs."

He got off his bike and helped me shove mine into the garage. Then he grinned down at me. "Thanks, Emmy. This was fun. I love a girl who can wrestle a double-dip sundae to the ground. Until tomorrow, then?"

The house felt funny just to walk into. From the hollow thump of his stereo through the floor, I knew Derek was up in his room. Mom and Dad were in the study with the door shut. Since I was too full of ice cream even to check the frig, I just went on upstairs. If parents don't care enough about a kid to see that she gets in at night, they deserve to have to look for her.

At the top of the stairs, I realized that Jayne must not have come in from her date with Geoff yet, because her door was open a little way and it was dark in there.

After setting out my yellow shorts and the biggest shirt I owned to wear to the frolic the next day, I went to bed and waited for Mom to come looking for me. I wondered if I should tell her that only Ben and I had gone for sundaes without Cassie's being along at all. Would it be like sneaking to go to the frolic with him when my folks just presumed I'd be with Cassie like always?

I felt shivery and funny because nobody even cared that I came home. At least this time I couldn't blame my strange feelings on that spooky, faceless doll in my closet. Somehow it had to be my own fault that I was the kind of kid nobody cared enough about even to check in at night.

I almost never dream. Cassie either dreams a lot of wonderful romantic stuff or makes it up to tell me. I used to dream I was being chased by bears, but that stopped when I was about ten. Since then, I have only waked up feeling I barely missed some shadowy thing that disappeared into the back of my mind. As they are always gone too quickly for me to recognize them, I can't say for certain those shadows are really dreams.

At first, I thought I was dreaming. There was a muffled jangling like a distant phone ringing, then a creaking noise. It sounded as if someone had walked on the third step from the bottom of the stairs. You can't get past it silently unless you just skip it and take two steps at a time. When Murph started barking out back, I knew I was awake and sat up. It was two in the morning by my new pink watch. My ears hurt from listening for things I didn't quite hear. I went to the window and looked out.

Our house is too far from the street light on the corner for me to recognize the cars parked out in front, but one of them was big and long, like the Wheaton car, and the other one shorter and brighter in color. From the fan of light spreading across the lawn, I knew the lamp was on in the study.

It didn't help any to watch those empty cars. I went to the bathroom so I could try to look into Jayne's room. It's worth my life to go in there without her asking me. Her door was closed and there wasn't any light showing under it. I stared and decided that didn't really mean anything. Jayne could be downstairs in the study with Dad, having one of those talks. At two in the morning?

Back in my bed, I tried to find a place where the sheet wasn't still hot from my lying there before. I didn't think I could possibly go to sleep, but I must have. The next things I heard were the cardinal singing, "*Wheet, wheet, cheedle, chew, pink,*" outside my window and Mom rapping on my door to wake me up.

I called to Mom that I was awake. Instead of going on downstairs, she opened the door and came in, carrying that hideous navy blue suitcase with the pigskin straps that she always packs for me.

"Emmy," she said, all breathless. "We've had a little change of plans."

I kept the sheet pulled up around my chin because I don't even want my own mother to see how bumpy I'm getting on my chest.

Mom is used to my not being a talker, but my silences make her cross, anyway. "Up, up!" she urged me. "You get to leave for Aunt Harriett's today instead of Friday afternoon. We need to get you packed."

"Why today?" I asked, not really believing her. This was the mother who collected perfect attendance records as if they were fine art. Did she really mean to pack me off with two days left—the All School Frolic and the closing assembly?

"You're going to enjoy this," she said, opening the suitcase on the foot of my bed and starting toward my dresser. "We got you an early flight out of Midway. You get to fly alone for the first time."

"But I have plans!" I wailed, remembering Ben.

She had piled my underwear in one corner of the suitcase and had opened my shorts drawer. "You'll have another All School Frolic next year," she reminded me. "And you know how you always hate the last day of school." Then she looked at me again. This time she smiled. "Aunt Harriett is really thrilled to have you come early. Aaron will pick you up at the airport in St. Louis and drive you home. But you're going to look pretty silly getting off the plane dragging that striped sheet. I think jeans would be more suitable than shorts to travel in."

All those phone calls, all these arrangements, and I hadn't even been asked. "Mom," I wailed. "I have plans, I really do. I don't *want* to miss the All School Frolic. I don't *want* to miss the last day of school."

Her back was to me. She stopped folding my shirts and stood very still. "Emmy," she said, very low and firm, as if she were talking to a real person instead of a kid. "All of us do things we don't want to do. I'm sorry, but that's how it is. Someday you'll understand."

I got to the door, still dragging my sheet, before I dared to answer back. "I want to understand *now*," I told her. "I want to understand why everybody acts so funny and why Jayne looks like a chicken and why it's always more convenient to ship me off than have me around." My breath came really funny because I don't usually get impudent out loud, no matter what I think to myself. She had turned and was staring at me. I don't cry easily because I work at it, but all of a sudden I was hot behind my eyes, which were leaking. "All my life I've been taken out to buy M&M's and I'm tired of it!"

She straightened up and stared at me with a look of astonished confusion. I left fast and banged the bathroom door behind me. I had blown it. I guess I shouldn't have put it that way, but she, of all people, should have understood what I meant.

Mom wheeled out the big gun while I was in the shower. I heard Dad calling through the door: "Hurry down, Emmy. I want to talk to you."

I tried to hurry, but crying makes my freckles look even worse than blushing does. He had poured my juice and was standing at the window of the back door, staring out into the yard.

"Sit down, Kitten," he said, taking the chair across from me. His face looked looser and older than it usually does. His eyes were dull, the way Jayne's had been. He didn't play any games with his voice but talked normally.

"I'm sorry you're upset, Emmy," he said, looking at his hands instead of my face. "There's a lot of stuff going on that needs our attention. We just decided you'd be better off not caught in the middle of it."

"Jayne's my sister," I told him. "I ought to know what's going on."

His eyes came up quickly. "And she's our

daughter," he reminded me. "If you were going through a painful problem, would you want us to make it public knowledge? The only thing you can do to help is go on down to Missouri and let us work this out."

I felt the orange juice stop halfway down my throat. In my mind I could see it in a big thick drop like a picture of motor oil on TV. His words played back through my mind, making me a little sick.

I was the one being robbed of the last two days of my seventh-grade life. *I* was the one being shipped off with only anger and confusion about the strange stuff coming down in our house. Yet he had managed to put me in the wrong in just two sentences. Guilt One: I was nosy and prying. Guilt Two: I was making things tougher for people. Guilt plus Guilt equals Villain.

"I need to make a phone call," I told him.

Startled and relieved, he nodded toward the phone.

Cassie's number is the only one I know by heart except my own. Lucky for me, Ben answered on the first ring. His voice sounded thick for a moment; then he swallowed whatever he was eating and said, "Emmy!" as if my voice were a nice surprise.

I couldn't get the words out. "I'm really sorry,"

I finally stammered. "I'm going to have to cancel today. I hope you don't mind."

Silence seems longer on a phone than on the air. "You okay?" he asked.

I nodded, then remembered to say, "Yes."

"I didn't do anything." He said it like a question.

"No," I said hastily. "Really, honest."

"Tell you what," he said in a hurried way. "Meet me at the back door. Okay? I'm gone." The phone clicked and the dial tone started. I clung to it anyway, wanting to call him back. But Murph began to bark and I knew it was pointless. Ben didn't letter in track by accident, and it doesn't take a sprinter like him very long to cross two back yards.

Because I was on the top step, I could see right into his eyes. I don't think very many people have eyes as blue as Ben's. He didn't wait for me to say anything.

"Three things," he said briskly. "Just nod if it's easier. Are you mad at me?"

I shook my head.

"Are you going to be around tonight when I come home?" I shook my head again and looked away because my eyes were really getting out of control.

"Missouri?" he asked. Then, when I nodded, "Does my motor-mouth sister have that address?"

"She does," I told him, wanting to wipe that serious look off his face. "And that was *four* things."

He smiled right into my face and said, "So who gave you permission to keep score?"

No boy has ever taken hold of my hands, both of them, the way he did then. It was a strange feeling, half scary and half wonderful. "I'm sorry," he said. "I'm really sorry about today. I was looking forward to it. But you have a good time and I'll write."

"Ben," I said, suddenly desperate about feeling in the dark when the sun was so bright that it made his hair look like cotton candy with a bright pink scalp underneath. "Do *you* know what's going on?"

He tightened his grip on my hands. "Not really, Emmy. I don't think anybody does for sure." He paused, his face reddening a little. "Please don't think I'm a nosy gossip like Cassie, but I did call Seth this morning. I saw the Wheaton car sitting with that unmarked cop car out in front of your place about two o'clock this morning and wondered. Geoff is missing, Emmy. Nobody's seen him since he took Jayne home about midnight. They haven't been able to find his car, either. Seth's dad thinks he might have run away or been kidnapped, they don't know which. Please don't say anything. I haven't told anybody but you."

I must have swayed a little bit from his words because he was gripping both of my arms tightly. He only let go when Dad came to the back door to call me inside.

8
Storm Front

$\mathcal{W}$e started for the airport before the buses even left the Junior High parking lot for the All School Frolic. Dad eased onto the Stevenson Expressway a little after nine, fitting his car in among the big semitrucks and yuppie compacts heading east for Chicago out of DuPage County. Since I didn't have anything to say and he didn't have any extra concentration left over from driving, we sat in silence.

Sitting there beside Dad, I remembered that in one more year I would have a learner's permit. Right then I didn't want to drive any more than I wanted to be thirteen. The decisions scared me. If you go at the speed limit on our roads, the cars swirl around you as if you were a rock in a stream. If you go with the flow, you run a fifty-fifty chance of being pulled over by one of the cops who huddle in under the overpasses with their radar guns trained on the innocent. Dad says a citation is twenty-five minutes and forty dollars he can't afford.

Dad checked his watch when we got off on Cicero Avenue and started watching the right side of the road. After a few blocks, he pulled off by a Convenience Store and asked me if I'd like a cold drink or anything. I shook my head. "They'll have stuff on the plane," I told him.

He nodded and got out, saying he'd be right back.

I couldn't see what was in the sack he set between us on the seat and I didn't ask him, but he carried it with him along with my suitcase into the airport.

As soon as the airline checked me in, Dad excused himself and went off to use the phone. I was the only kid in the waiting area, and there weren't even very many women. Mostly it was men in business suits with briefcases, their heads hidden in the morning paper. As Dad walked toward me, he looked old and tense and upset. When he saw me watching him, his face deliberately brightened and he smiled.

"We could have some weather before this day's through," he told me, taking the seat next to mine.

I just looked at him because, whatever it was, we were bound to have *some* kind of weather, if only to keep the TV weather people employed. He knows enough about the way I think that he laughed. "All right, Emmy," he said with a little chuckle. "I don't know who appointed you editor of the world, but you're right. I mean, you could have some *real* weather. According to the map in the *Trib* this morning, there's a storm front moving this way. It will hit your Aunt Harriett's place before it gets here."

"I hope it doesn't spoil the All School Frolic," I said, without thinking. That nice magic moment of our appreciating each other was gone as fast as it had come. He looked strange and fell silent until the stewardess called us to load.

Dad walked with me clear to the ramp, then handed me the package. He spoke quickly, as if he hadn't left himself enough time for all he had to say. "Kiss Aunt Harriett for me," he said. "And this is from your mom. She said she finally figured out what you meant and some day she'll be able to explain."

After a hug, I went into that boarding tunnel, which is like a slinky in a paper wrapping. The limp way the thing in the sack lopped over my hand told me it was one of those big cellophane bags of candy that they sell in theater lobbies. After I fastened my seat belt I looked at it. It wasn't M&M's or gummy bears this time but Hershey kisses, ten and a half ounces, packaged to look like a pound.

When I don't see someone for a while, I forget how much I like them. Because of his jeans jacket and ponytail, Aaron stood out in the crowd waiting at the gate. His smile was outstanding, too, and my heart leaped up a little because he was my friend.

"Good flight?" he asked as we started for the baggage claim area. I didn't have to tell him which bag was mine. He remembered and pulled it off as soon as it came through the chute.

When Aaron started across the parking lot with my bag, I thought about Ben and the way he had opened doors for me and put my bike away without asking. It didn't seem right for Aaron to haul my bag through the lot when I was perfectly able to carry it myself and he had that old war injury that gave him a rolling walk like Popeye in the cartoon.

"I can carry that," I told him.

"So can I," he replied, nodding toward the lane where he had parked.

The inside of Aunt Harriett's station wagon smelled ferocious. "Rufus," Aaron explained, when he saw my expression. "He crawls up and sleeps in the back end, hoping for a free ride to anywhere. I dragged him out whining when I started here today."

I felt a little curl of excitement. I'd been so confused and annoyed the past few days, it hadn't really dawned on me that I was almost at Aunt Harriett's. Getting into that station wagon with a handful of sunflower seeds loose in the back seat and the Rufus smell choking me suddenly made it real.

"How is Aunt Harriett?" I asked, rolling my window all the way down.

His smile was sudden and brilliant. "It really perked her up to hear that you were coming early."

I looked at him. What was he talking about? Aunt Harriett was always perky. He glanced at me sideways. "Didn't your folks tell you she's been feeling poorly on and off ever since Easter?"

A quick surge of anger got between me and my manners. "My parents," I said stiffly, "are not into telling me anything."

I saw him glance at me and frown. "So I gather," he said. "In this case, they're wrong. She could have one of her spells while you're here. She's always fine after a while but I wouldn't want you to be scared."

"What kind of spells?" I asked, suddenly shivery again inside. Nothing could be wrong with Aunt Harriett! It couldn't. I wouldn't let it.

"Something I never heard of before," he said. "Doc Hollis uses the initials TIA. If I understood what he told me, little blood vessels break inside her brain. She's confused for a while, and scared. Then she can't remember what happened. Once she gets a good sleep, she feels okay."

I leaned my head back against the seat and looked out the window. Maybe I'd dreaded the wrong things about being thirteen. With all my fretting about myself, I hadn't figured on the people in my life being changed—Jayne, Cassie, now Aunt Harriett.

Right away, St. Louis was all the way behind us. The breath from the fields and woods swept the car clean of Rufus smell. Masses of black-eyed Susans turned the roadside to gold, with patches of white here and there from Queen Anne's lace. (Back home, the open spaces were blue and purple with chicory and wild phlox.) Strands of swiftly moving clouds laced the sky, which had been a clear, open blue when my plane landed.

"You okay?" Aaron asked, glancing over at me.

"Growing up is the pits," I told him, not even trying to keep the anger out of my voice.

"You've been brainwashed," he said, without taking his eyes off the road.

"I have not," I told him hotly. "I'd rather die than grow up."

He chuckled. "That's about your only choice."

"There's nothing funny about it," I almost snapped. "I hate growing up. I hate having the best years of my life behind me."

"Who's been giving you that?" he asked, sounding annoyed.

"Everybody," I said. Then I mimicked the way I had heard people say it: "Oh, to be a child again."

"Then *everybody* needs to have their mouths washed out with soap for bald-faced lying," he said.

He didn't have to be rude! I glared at him. "Tell me one good thing about growing up," I challenged.

"Easy," he said, looking over at me. "Control. Growing up gives you the right to call your own shots. Now hang on. The spring rains play hob with this road. It's as spiny as a warthog to get over."

He turned off the highway to wind along the rocky, twisting lane that leads up to Aunt Harriett's house. At first you see only the chimneys, perched like brick hats on the top of the woods. Then you turn a corner and the whole house appears, sudden and overwhelming with its porches fanning out like aprons and its windows mirrored with sunlight.

That was only a moment. I was still staring at it when a cloud passed over and the whole house darkened before my eyes.

"Storm coming," Aaron said, pulling up in front of the door. "You scat on inside. I'll bring your stuff after I put this wagon away."

He paused and looked at me intently. "Make as if you can't tell any difference in your aunt, okay?"

Aunt Harriett's housekeeper, Maudie, is afraid of everything. Aunt Harriett says Maudie's world closes in on her because she won't stiffen her spine and push it back.

Once Derek and I made an alphabet of the things we'd heard Maudie say "gave her the willies."

Ants.

Bugs—no matter how many wings or legs they have.

Cats—that roam around and get rabies.

Dogs—that get rabies from cats.

Eggs—that give you salmonella unless they're cooked as hard as leather.

Foxes—back to rabies again.

We'd gotten bored long before we reached the letter *S*, but Maudie was *really* afraid of storms.

When one caught her at the house, she'd run down in the cellar to sit with her apron over her face and moan.

Aunt Harriett had sent Maudie on home when the clouds started moving in. Before she left, Maudie had set out a tray of roast beef sandwiches with sweet pickles laid on top and raw vegetables. The cake stand was piled high with those spicy bar cookies with raisins and nuts inside and a clear icing you can see through.

Aaron came in as Aunt Harriett poured hot water into the Blue Onion pot to make tea.

"Did I bring the right kid?" he asked.

Aunt Harriett laughed softly. "Not only the right one, but I do like her in this new, large, economy-size package. Or have I shrunk since Easter?"

She *had* shrunk. She was not only shorter but more fragile looking, as if even her bones had lost weight. But her eyes were bright behind her delicate, wire-rimmed glasses, and her hair was a rebellion of white curls trying to escape from a twisted knot. "I've grown," I assured her. "In all directions." I didn't mention the bumps.

She smiled, then held up her hand for silence. "This storm is about to hit, Aaron. Maybe you should see to the windows while the tea is brewing."

Aaron rose and started toward the front of the house. "Be sure there are candles in all our rooms," she called after him. "It's going to be a lot darker before it's light again."

The leaves of the black walnut tree by the porch whipped against a milky sky. The sky darkened as we ate, and the thunder, which had been only a sullen growling, began to explode in sudden, deafening crashes. When Aaron came back from letting a quivering Rufus into the cellar, his shirt had dollar-size wet spots from the rain that had begun to drum against the window. Soon water was springing from the downspouts to flow in swift streams across the yard.

By the time we finished eating, the electrical part of the storm had passed, but the rain still fell steadily, rhythmic against the windows and the roof.

Aaron looked over at Aunt Harriett and laughed. "If I ever saw a pair of eyelids drooping toward a nap, they're yours," he told her. "Emmy and I will take over here in the kitchen."

Aunt Harriett rose. "We *all* love a rainy afternoon," she said. "I'll take you up on that offer." The way she said that "all" made me shiver a little.

Aaron left the room with her but came right back.

"I thought you went upstairs," I told him.

He shook his head and snapped on the little portable TV. "I just watch her safely up the steps whenever I can."

The hands of the wooden-framed schoolhouse clock above the refrigerator stood at two-thirty. Our All School Frolic would be winding down, with most of the kids just piled on the grass watching a few diehards play softball. I wondered if Cassie had "pranced around," as Ben put it, with Scott Lerner, having a glorious time showing off. Had Ben really missed me as he said he would?

The TV announcer reported that a tornado had touched down near a small Oklahoma town and that a storm warning would remain in effect until nine that evening.

The announcer went from the weather into the news without missing a breath. "Chicago area police have launched an intensive search for the missing son of a well-known Chicago attorney."

Aaron reached for the button, but I caught his hand.

"Police and friends have been unable to find any trace of Geoff Wheaton, eighteen-year-old son of Allan R. Wheaton of Oakbrook, who was last seen at about midnight, Wednesday, the tenth of June, when he dropped off his girl companion at her home in Hinsdale."

Aaron watched my face as the report came to a close.

"Jayne?" he asked.

I nodded.

"Your folks meant well," he said. "And your being here sure gives your Aunt Harriett a boost."

I leaned on my hands at the sink with the noises of the night before replaying in my mind—the phone ringing, Murph barking, someone on the stairs—and the cars sitting silently out in front. Ben had called the small car "an unmarked cop car."

Always before this, my parents' hidden troubles had been things that didn't touch the core of my life—that business of Dad's having to find a new job, the time my Aunt Linda lost a baby before it was ready to be born, the stroke my grandmother had suffered off in Arizona and later died from. This was Jayne, my Jayne.

Aaron brought me back by tossing the wet dish towel so swiftly that I almost didn't move in time to catch it.

I turned and stared at him. "How much do you know about this business with Jayne and Geoff Wheaton?" I asked.

He shrugged. "More than you do, I guess, but not enough to understand it."

I give Aaron points. When he wants to get

94

away, he moves fast. He pulled a hooded slicker from a hook in the back hall and let himself out into the rain before I could ask my next question.

Outside the rain still hammered against the house. I was alone in there with Aunt Harriett and her sleeping ghosts.

9
Chlorophyll

Aunt Harriett had been wrong about her ghosts all liking rainy-day naps. I lay on my stomach in the blue room I had always shared with Jayne and listened to the sounds in the old house as I watched the rain flatten itself against the window glass and leak down like tears.

Because Aunt Harriett had talked so much to me about her beloved family ghosts, I could sort out the noises she attributed to them. It wasn't windy enough to hear the Captain drag his peg leg around, but the piano downstairs tinkled a broken tune just as if Aunt Ida were whiling away the afternoon there. A door somewhere slammed. That would be Uncle Paris.

Derek can give you an explanation for every sound you hear in that house. I don't know whether he figured all that stuff out to keep from being afraid himself or if he really doesn't believe in anything like that.

In any case, as I listened to the sounds in the house that afternoon, I thought of his "logic," as he calls it.

Derek scoffed the most at the thought of the old Captain dragging his peg leg along. "Aunt Harriett says herself you never hear him except when the wind blows. Look at this place with all its wooden shutters and balconies and gingerbread trim. Any loose piece of wood will make that scraping noise when the wind blows on it."

Aunt Harriett remembers Aunt Ida, who came to live in the house when Aunt Harriett was just a little kid. According to Aunt Harriett, Aunt Ida, who'd been a singer on a showboat on the Mississippi River, was courted by rich, handsome men from New Orleans to St. Louis. But, since she never found a gentleman who was the match of her father, she died a maiden, playing his favorite song on the old spinet in the library downstairs.

Derek says what we hear is only the vibration

of the wires in the old piano that hasn't been tuned for fifty years at least. He may be right, but I know for sure that the music isn't the same all the time. When it sounds slow and sad, Aunt Harriett gets fretful and prepares herself for grief. Mostly, however, the rhythm from the piano is light and soft, like a love song or a lullaby. Then Aunt Harriett smiles and hums to herself.

Uncle Paris, who was Aunt Harriett's husband, is the youngest of the ghosts and my favorite one to hear stories about. He's the one who opens and closes doors at all hours, day and night. Derek says that the old house has settled on its cliff, making the doors hang loose so that the slightest breeze will make them chatter.

When Derek told Aunt Harriett that, she smiled and touched the sapphire ring Uncle Paris gave her when he went away to fight in World War I. After the Armistice in 1919, she took a train to New York City to meet his ship. They got married before they even left New York. After the war, Uncle Paris was always a light sleeper. Instead of tossing and turning as some might do, he walked the house, guarding it like the sentry he had been along the trenches in France. Death had not been enough to take him away from Aunt Harriett or change his habits.

I drifted off to sleep and waked up with a start. It was dark outside. I sat up and hugged my knees. The buses had taken everybody back from the All School Frolic by now. The police were looking for Geoff Wheaton. My parents hadn't even called to see if I'd arrived safely. For all they knew, my plane could have gone down and people were poking around in the wreckage, trying to find the pilot's black box and identify my bones.

Aunt Harriett was already downstairs when I got there. My thank-you note had come in the afternoon mail. She held it close to the light and read it carefully. Then she crossed her hands over it in her lap and smiled. "I knew you would know why I sent you that doll, Emmy. I'm glad you like it."

Through that evening, which lasted forever, I fought a losing battle against myself. I was tense and angry and confused in a dozen different ways. Aunt Harriett got sleepy again right after dinner and went to bed early. I watched the news. They reported no progress in the hunt for Geoff Wheaton, and they used more expensive air time talking about his father than they did about him.

I wanted to call home but didn't. Instead, I watched an old movie on Maudie's little TV in the kitchen. Movies never bore me. This one did. I finally went to bed, only to be waked up trembling from my first nightmare. I had dreamed that Ben Malone was missing, and I cried myself back to sleep.

I woke Friday knowing that it was final assembly day in Hinsdale. Cassie would be sitting with Scott Lerner and making fun of everything anybody else did. Ben, blushing almost as pink as his hair, would go up to the platform time after time for one award after another, because he was good at most everything. I wished I were there to clap for him.

And that wasn't all. It wasn't Cassie I was missing but her brother Ben. Fresh confusion! I have known Ben ever since I can remember. Was I being a weird teenager and kidding myself that I liked Ben just because he had been so awfully nice to me?

Sweetness and light, the kid's world. And under and beneath it all, terrifying things were happening in my family's life. Was it because nobody seemed to want me that my family filled my mind? I kept seeing Jayne's huge eyes, anguished and dull, and remembering that funny, awkward business of Mom sending me a bag of candy and saying she finally understood. I'd even thought of Derek a few times, and that was something I usually avoided in the interest of my mental health.

In the few short days that had passed since the Sunday Doll arrived by special post, my life had neatly landed in a cocked hat. And dear, sweet Aunt Harriett had mentioned the doll in a way that kept me from asking what it meant.

I worked my way through Friday, killing time one painful hour after another. It was weird to be at Aunt Harriett's and have my mind back home. Usually it's the other way around. When Aunt Harriett went upstairs for her nap I even thought about watching TV, which I never do in the daytime at her house. But Maudie was using the little portable in the kitchen, sniffling her way through a soap opera.

The minute I went out on the back steps, Rufus saw me and came bounding up. "What happened?" I asked him, actually leaning over to touch him. "You don't even stink."

"I washed him," Aaron called from the other side of the smokehouse, where I couldn't see him. When I walked around there, Rufus came too, wagging wildly under my hand. "Aren't you going to ask why I washed him?" Aaron prodded.

"I probably don't want to know," I said. "Tell me anyway."

Aaron was kneeling beside the asparagus bed, which is made of clean river sand framed by boards. He grinned up at me. "Like someone else I could mention, Rufus was overwhelmed by his own nosiness. He found something dead—an elephant, from the smell of it—and rolled in it."

I squatted beside Aaron. A colander on the ground was half full of fat white asparagus rods about four inches long. The asparagus stalks in the markets at home are either long and thin like flexible pencils or fat like skinny hot dogs, but they're always green.

As I watched, Aaron slid his index finger down into the sand and broke off another stalk.

"Why isn't it green?" I asked.

"See what I mean about nosy?" he said. "Because the sun hasn't touched it yet. It doesn't take on its real color until it's out in the world on its own. Chlorophyll."

I nodded. I won my red ribbon at the Science Fair with an experiment showing how bean sprouts turn green because of chlorophyll. It was fascinating to see somebody turning the tables on the sun like that. Then, forgetting his teasing about my nosiness, I asked. "Where did you learn to grow asparagus like that?"

"From the same woman who taught me to clean

garden snails for the table. Want to pick some?" He guided my finger down a stalk and told me to push against its base when my finger touched hard ground. I felt the snap of the crisp stalk through my skin.

He stood up to watch me. "This woman was French and very picky about her food. I built a bed like this for her and filled it with sand from the beach."

I heard his smile change his voice. "Want to know how to get the green out of snails so you can cook them with garlic butter?"

"No." I groaned at the thought. Then I laughed. "See? I'm not as nosy as you thought."

He scoffed. "You were *born* nosy. I've heard about your first trip here." He picked up the colander. "The rest of those stalks won't be ready until tomorrow. We'll have a big batch by the time your folks come down this weekend."

"What if they don't come?" I challenged him.

"Do you want to hear about your first trip here or not?" he asked.

Hearing stories about yourself before you can remember makes you feel real. "So I was nosy," I prodded him.

He looked at me without seeing me. I knew he was looking through me to another time, the way adults do. "You and your family still lived in Connecticut when your Uncle Paris died."

I nodded. I don't remember Aunt Harriett's husband, but Dad has told me a lot about him. He was very tall, and straight backed to his grave. His hair and mustache were white, and he had a great beak of a nose that he sheltered under the brim of a Panama hat. I imagine him looking like the picture of Mark Twain in the front of my *Huckleberry Finn*. Aunt Harriett said he was a "gentleman by nature and a horse breeder by trade."

"Your Aunt Harriett was desolate when he died," Aaron went on. "Wouldn't leave her bedroom or eat a bite. Your dad came out for the funeral but only brought you with him. The other kids were sick, chicken pox, as I recall. You were barely walking but full of the devil."

I knew this story. I'd pried the top off the beehive with a stick and brought the bees swarming after me to the back door. "I guess I just wanted to see inside a bee house," I told him.

"Nosy," he corrected me, then laughed. "Your aunt said she was lying down with her eyes shut when it happened. She felt this pluck on her sleeve, the way your Uncle Paris used to waken her. She sat up all trembling, certain he was warning her of something. She flew to her bedroom window and saw that cloud of bees chasing you. That brought her down, you bet! She put so much soda on your stings that they had to go to the store before they could make biscuits again."

He smiled at me and I grinned back. I've seen pictures of myself then, and the scene is as plain to me as if I had watched it in a movie.

"But it wasn't just the bees that kept your aunt moving," Aaron went on. "You went from one piece of mischief to another like a lapful of eels. She just gave up on dying of grief, deciding to hang around to see what you'd turn into. If you survived, that is."

We had walked to the house. Aaron handed me the colander at the kitchen door. Inside, the phone was ringing. Maudie took it and then waggled her arm in my direction to signal that the call was for me.

10
The First Phone Call

I went in expecting that call to be from home. When I heard Cassie's voice instead, I was just struck dumb.

"Emmy," she called. "Are you there? Emmy?"

"I'm here," I finally said. Maybe Aaron is right. Maybe I am nosy. All I could do was wonder why she was calling me long distance like this when the cheaper evening rates hadn't begun yet. She sounded excited and pumped up, not the way I like her the best.

"They found him," she said, all in a rush. "They found Geoff Wheaton hanged by the neck in one of those hay sheds over by his parents' stable. He *killed* himself!"

I couldn't stand what she was saying. Waves of shock trembled all the way down my body. But even as I stood there, bracing for my own balance, I realized that the way her voice sounded—eager and excited, sort of wet-mouthed and greedy—was making my stomach heave with nausea.

When I didn't say anything, she started yelling at me again as if the phone line wasn't there and she could shout all the way from Chicago. "Emmy!" she said. "Didn't you hear me? Say something, Emmy. Are you there? He's dead. Geoff Wheaton is dead and they're calling it suicide. Your sister Jayne's picture was on TV."

I set the phone back on the hook and walked outside blindly. Rufus bounded over and started slobbering at my hands. Aaron was putting away his tools. He stopped with a rake in his hand and leaned on it, staring at me. I shook my head, feeling my sudden tears flying sideways into my hair.

I wanted to tear at my eyes, not because of the tears but because of what Cassie's words had made me see.

I know those hay sheds. One year the All School Frolic was held out there. We climbed into carts of hay that were waiting in the school parking lot. It wasn't altogether fun. The hay crept up under my shorts and itched me where I couldn't scratch in public. It left me with a rash that didn't clear up for almost a week.

The two hay sheds were back behind the Wheaton stables in a grove of trees. When you got inside, the sheds were big and open and dark from the overhanging trees. The air inside smelled of summer, like freshly mowed grass drying in the sun. Birds darted and chittered up in the high, arched eaves, which were crusted with little dried nests made out of mud. The kids had argued about whether the birds were swifts or barn swallows.

In spite of their being dark and big, the sheds seemed to be filled with life. Mice rustled in the straw, and pillars of insects swayed in and out the glassless windows on humming errands from one mound of horse dung to another. The high corners where the sun didn't reach were draped with spider webs that were absolutely huge. Some were old and worn out, so loaded with dust that strands had broken free to sway in the air.

It wasn't my eyes I needed to tear at, but my brain. Why was my head filled with a picture of how Geoff looked, limp, with his shoulders folded in and his head on his chest, oddly to one side? Only his clothes were wrong.

Geoff had always been what Cassie called "a dresser," but, in the picture scalding my mind, Geoff's clothes were dark and rumpled and shapeless. His hands hung loose and white against his thighs. I knew my crazy, scrambled head was throwing the wrong pictures at me, pictures from old movies where bad men had been hanged on bare, open scaffolds in unpainted towns with dirt streets and storefronts that were just boards stuck up to make the buildings look taller than they really were.

But those dead men had been bad men, criminals who had fought against the law and lost.

Geoff Wheaton wasn't bad. What law had he ever broken? He was just an ordinary kid who hadn't made the greatest scores on his SATs and got caught in what Ben had called a "pressure cooker."

"Emmy," Aaron called. "Are you all right?"

I nodded, still stumbling away without even knowing where I was headed. The afternoon sun buttered the heaps of grass Aaron had mowed in the meadow. I startled a meadow lark that began to pip and flop away, pretending she had a broken wing so I would go after her instead of her hidden nest.

The smell of the hay came full at me without warning, reminding me of the Wheaton hay barn, and I began to vomit.

I don't know how Aaron got to water and back that fast but he was there, squatting beside me, forcing my head down between my knees with a cold cloth pressed against my eyes. My stomach finally quit cramping and I shuddered.

"Thanks," I told him, my voice coming funny because my nose was full of vomit.

"Best move to the shade," he said.

He walked beside me. He didn't touch me, but I knew he was there if I stumbled. When we got to the cottonwood tree, I slid down the trunk and leaned back against it. "Thanks again," I said. "I'm really sorry."

He handed me the wet handkerchief he had pressed on my head and I blew my nose. He hunkered with his knees bent, a little way away. "I'm sorry, too," he said. "Better now?"

I nodded my head. As much as I hated and despised and loathed Cassie Malone for calling to tell me that news, and the greedy awful way her voice had sounded, I was somehow compelled to tell Aaron.

"Geoff Wheaton is dead," I said.

Aaron's hands are shaped a lot like my dad's, square and strong with long fingers, but Aaron's hands are stained from use. His right hand trembled as he plucked a strand of grass and put it in his mouth to chew on.

"Suicide," I whispered after a minute.

I always think of Aaron as being a lot like I am only older and a man instead of a girl. Neither of us are really talkers and neither of us go in for those big scenes that people like Cassie and Derek do. I caught my breath, half scared, when Aaron leaped to his feet with a roar almost like that of an animal. I didn't catch what he was saying at first, but the word was "Waste!"

He screamed it over and over, pounding his fists against the trunk of the cottonwood tree as if he could knock it over where it stood. Dry shreds of bark tore loose and showered into the grass around me at the base of the tree.

"Aaron," I cried, scrambling to my feet. "Please, Aaron."

He didn't even seem to hear me until I caught at his arm, digging in with my fingernails, trying to make him stop before he hammered the skin off his hands right down to the bones and blood.

He stopped at my touch and pressed his fists hard against the tree for a minute without looking around. When he turned toward me, he was shaking all over and his head drooped like the picture of Geoff in my mind.

"Emmy," he said heavily. "God, what a world we live in! Poisoned earth and poisoned air and wasted, wasted lives."

He started walking back to the house in an awkward, shambling way and I fell in beside him, having to force my legs along because of a sudden tiredness deep inside my bones.

"At least he's out of it, poor devil," he mumbled. "He can't be hurt any more."

"Don't say that, Aaron," I cried. "That's an awful thing to say."

He shook his head. "It's true, Emmy. That kid is past pain, but he's about the only one. It isn't death that's bad—death is a perfectly normal piece of the life package. What's bad is the way the living deal with it. It's like a rock thrown in water. When that stone sinks, it makes waves. How do you think that boy's family is going to deal with what they pushed him to? Will Jayne ever get past thinking of Geoff and asking herself if she could have saved his life by doing what he wanted her to?"

I shook my head. "I don't understand."

He glanced at me and ruffled up my hair the way he does Rufus' coat. "I forgot. They were trying to shelter you, weren't they? Your dad spilled the whole story out to Aunt Harriett when he called about sending you down here. Poor Geoff. They had him against the wall, I guess. The only escape he could see was to marry Jayne and run away where he could start again on his own. He just wanted to be with somebody who cared about *him* and liked him the way he was, instead of trying to force him into some other mold. Your Aunt Harriett told your dad he was making a mistake by not telling you what was going on, but he didn't pay any attention to her. Even if they *had* been able to shield you until now, Geoff has put a stop to that."

I was still trying to absorb what he had said. "That's crazy!" I cried. "Jayne hasn't even finished her schooling."

"Sure it was crazy," he nodded. "Jayne knew that as well as anybody. But what do you do when somebody you love is crying out for help and nobody else is listening?"

Maudie was hooting from the back door, waving her apron to get our attention. "Emmy!" she called. "Your folks are on the line."

"It's too late," I told Aaron. "I don't want to talk to them."

He looked at me with his head a little bit on the side. "What good will that do, Emmy? All you can do is make it even worse for your parents. Don't you think they've figured out how bad they've blown it with you? Grow up. Be generous. Let them off the hook."

[There wasn't any movie in my memory with

113

a shot of a stone falling into water and sending waves crashing out to drown all those people: Geoff's folks in their long black car, Jayne sobbing helplessly into a pillow in her dark room, Mom wailing in the dark of the back yard, "I don't know what to do."]

I started for the house at a run because time passes so slowly when you're waiting on a phone. Rufus thought it was a game and raced me, his tongue spraying spit as it swayed back and forth from the side of his mouth.

11
And the Second

I was breathless by the time I got to the phone.

"Well, finally," Dad said. "Where were you, anyway?"

"Out in back with Aaron," I told him. "How's Jayne?"

A little silence. "Why, she's fine, Emmy. More to the point, how's Aunt Harriett?"

Then the game still wasn't over.

A cold kind of anger settled into my chest. I could hear it in my own voice but I couldn't do anything about it. "Aunt Harriett's fine right now,

Dad. Why didn't you tell me she's been having these spells?"

His concern was quick and earnest. "Has she had another one? How is she, really?"

"She's fine," I repeated. "Why didn't you tell me she was having these spells?"

"What could you have done about it except be upset?" he asked, bridling a little as he tried to shove me back into the helplessness of being a kid.

"I could have *cared*," I told him angrily.

His sigh came clearly over the wire. "Let's not start that again, Emmy. I called to tell you that we won't be able to make it on Saturday as we planned. We'll let you know as soon as we are able to get away and come down.'

Aaron had followed me into the kitchen. He was standing in the doorway, openly listening. Maudie, feeling the tension, fiddled with her apron and looked from one of us to the other. *Be generous*, Aaron had told me. *Let them off the hook.*

But they were the ones who had made the hook, not me. It had been *their* idea to push me out, wall me away, ship me off. Good old business as usual, and talk happy for the kid. They'd made the hook and caught themselves on it.

Aaron's face was as carefully blank as that of the Sunday Doll. He wasn't out to live my life for me. But his words had a way of sticking in my head like a goat's head thorn in a sock. *Control*, Aaron had said. *What you get when you grow up is control.*

I sure turned down a lot of choices in that split second. I didn't tell Dad that I knew Geoff was dead and Jayne was being swept away by waves of guilt. I didn't tell him that I had already realized they wouldn't come after me until the whole business of Geoff's death was as settled as death ever is. I didn't even tell him to thank Mom for the chocolate kisses because that would have been a twist on the hook, too.

Instead, I caught my breath hard and tried to pull the hook out as gently as I could.

"Come whenever you can, Dad," I told him. "You know I always love being here." After a final flurry of wordy affection singing over the wires, we both hung up our phones.

I gave Maudie one of those smiles that I had promised myself I would never make my mouth form except in self-defense. "I hope everybody is really hungry for asparagus," I told her. "My folks can't make it this weekend. They'll call when they can."

I walked outside with my feet feeling funny, as if they had gone flat and huge and heavy like Charlie Chaplin clown feet. Aaron followed. "That's all?" he asked, more surprise in his voice than I had ever heard. "He just called to say they aren't coming down this weekend?"

Bless Aaron. When I nodded, he laughed.

We sat down on the railroad tie that separates the end of the garden from the beginning of the yard. A crazy zucchini squash plant with a mob of yellow blossoms was spilling over, trying to pretend it was grass. Aaron lifted it gently and put it back in place. One of Aunt Harriett's cardinals hopped along the porch rail, sang a couple of repeats, then cocked his head to examine us.

"Wonder he doesn't laugh instead of singing," Aaron said. "We're a pretty disreputable-looking pair."

We were, him with his beard that needed a trim and hair every kind of length held tight by a leather shoelace. I was no better, with my freckles two shades darker from crying and vomit stains on my shirt.

For some reason, time felt suddenly limp and endless, like those transition scenes in a movie when the camera drops to slow motion and pans the scenery on its way to the next dramatic scene. You know you're going to be into it again right away, but you grab that little breather and hang on. I thought about Ben and tried to imagine him sitting there with Aaron and me. Aaron wouldn't think Ben was funny looking, even if he'd never seen a boy with almost pink hair before. Aaron would look right past that and see Ben, loose and honest and kind, the way I see him. And Ben would like Aaron, too, I was sure of that. The peace of that minute gave me the nerve to ask Aaron something I had wondered about a lot of times.

"How did you end up here?"

"The same way you did. Luck," he told me.

"I was born into this family," I reminded him.

"You don't call that luck?" He fished in the grass for a blade of green to chew on. "Maybe your folks *have* put you through some tough times, but they never meant to. They were only trying to protect you—to give you the perfect childhood. You could have gotten folks who didn't *care* what happened to you—how hard you got hit, or by whom."

He tossed the ragged grass away. "Let's say that it was my luck to be a foundling. Your Aunt Harriett found me in her barn loft, an innocent, helpless babe of twenty-seven who needed to give up his bottle and have some breathing space."

From the way he got up and hitched his jeans, I knew that was all I was going to hear. He looked down at me. "She'll be waking up now, and we're

119

bound to tell her about your sister's friend. If we don't, she'll pick it up some other way and take it a lot harder."

"We?" I echoed hopefully.

He shrugged. "Most jobs go easier with two sets of hands on the saw."

When I passed Aunt Harriett's room to change my clothes, she called out to me. "About ready for tea, Emmy?" she asked.

"Aaron's got the kettle on already," I told her.

By the time I pulled on a fresh shirt, she was waiting in the hall. I giggled. She was wearing a soft blue cotton dress printed all over with tiny white flowers. You couldn't see her legs at all between the hem and her scarred, yellow-leather hiking boots. As if that wasn't strange enough, she was dangling her big straw hat at her side by its ribbons.

"It's rude to laugh at your elders," she told me, glancing down at her boots. Then she grinned up at me. "Sloth lazy, that's what I am. Those very early yellow apples should be ripening this week. I thought we'd go pick some after tea and decided to save a trip back up here to change my shoes."

By the time we reached the lower hall, the kettle was working itself up to a full screech. Aunt Harriett paused, cocked her head, and looked up at me. "What's wrong, Emmy?" she asked. "Why do I have the feeling that something's terribly wrong?"

Aaron spoke from the kitchen door. "Emmy got a call from her dad while you were napping," he told her. "Come on, you two."

I looked past her to meet Aaron's eyes and saw him waggle his head toward the library where the old piano stood. You couldn't hear a tune, only the kind of a broken, stuttering rhythm that was anything but happy.

Aunt Harriett sat with her hands folded together on the kitchen table while we told her about Geoff. I was careful with words, maybe too careful, because she studied my face intently when I gave her Dad's message. "Your father told you about this boy?" she asked.

My glance at Aaron was a plain appeal for help. He was ready. "One of Emmy's friends called about Geoff," he explained. "She went out of her way to dump the bad news on Emmy. She did it in the worst possible way, I might add. Your nephew only called to say they wouldn't be down this weekend."

Aunt Harriett shook her head with a flip of irritation. "I refuse to apologize for that nephew of mine, but he can be a real impediment sometimes."

She leaned to take one of my hands. "The waste of this death breaks my heart. What kind of a boy was Geoff Wheaton?"

I caught my breath hard. He's always been Geoff, hyphen, wimp, in my mind. "I don't think he ever got a chance to find out," I told her.

"But Jayne loved him?"

When I nodded, she sighed. "The shortest lives cast the longest shadows," she said. "It's the waste."

I usually take milk or lemonade. That day I took tea and held the cup up close to inhale its pungent steam. "You'll have a job getting your sister through this," Aunt Harriett said after a minute.

I stared at her. "Me?" I asked with a startled squeak.

She nodded. "Jayne won't be able to get on top of this until she finds herself a whole lot better than she has yet. She'll need help doing that."

My first impulse was to rush to Jayne's defense, to tell Aunt Harriett that my sister was just fine the way she was. Then I caught myself, remembering how cross I've been with her since she started being the state-of-the-art teenager instead of her old self.

Surely Aunt Harriett didn't think *I* could help Jayne! "But—" I began, ready to argue how little attention Jayne paid to me, what a kid she thought I was.

Aunt Harriett shook her head, cutting me off. "The weak turn to the strong," she said. "She'll be able to see your real face now. I'm right, aren't I, that you really do love her?"

Did I love Jayne? What kind of a question was that? For a blinding second there I hated Aunt Harriett for asking. For the first time since Cassie's call, I put my head down and really bawled.

Aaron tried to talk Aunt Harriett out of going to the orchard to pick apples.

"You look peaky," he told her.

"And you look scruffy," she answered tartly. "Stay here if you want. Emmy and I can go alone."

He grinned and went to the storage house for buckets.

Rufus bounded out of the back of the station wagon and galloped over as we left the house. He raced ahead of us, chairman in charge of everything that could be flushed from the brush. You couldn't hear yourself think over the chattering of the squirrels that he sent into frenzies of foul language.

One of Aunt Harriett's cardinals hopped along behind us to the second fence. I listened a little critically to his song. My cardinal back home still sang the sweetest I'd heard. "That's an old bird," Aunt Harriett told me. "He remembers the seeds of many a winter."

The orchard grass had been battered into wet green dunes by the storm of the day before. The lower branches of the early-bearing tree were weighted down with pale yellow apples. Aunt Harriett picked one, brushed off a fruit fly, wiped it on her skirt, and took a big bite.

"Mush!" she said, spitting it out at once. "How can the world's best sauce apple be so nasty to eat raw? Let's take as many as we can carry, Aaron. I can smell the cinnamon of that applesauce already."

We had filled Aaron's buckets and were starting back when Aunt Harriett suddenly stopped. Her gloved hand groped for me and missed. I turned and heard her give out a queer, strangled cry. I hope some day I can forget how her face looked, slack and pale, her mouth a gaping triangle and her eyes not focused. Aaron let the buckets fly and caught her halfway to the ground.

"Hollis," he told me. "The doctor's name is Hollis. Tell him to get himself out here on the double and not to try that ambulance business on you."

I was rooted. Aaron's legs were widespread to

brace himself against Aunt Harriett's weight. "Hollis, Emmy," he repeated. "Move."

The woman on the phone was impossible. "Listen, honey," she kept saying. "Let me talk to a member of the family."

"I *am* the family," I told her, repeating Aunt Harriett's name and the directions for the second time.

"I'll send an ambulance." She tried again, just as I heard the thump of Aaron's boot kicking against the back door to signal me to let him in.

"We don't want an ambulance," I told her, my voice rising. "Send the doctor. Now!"

"Look, child," she said, clearly beginning to lose her temper. "My husband is out running his daily five miles. I can get an ambulance out there within minutes."

"*Find him*," I told her, hanging up the phone to go open the door.

I walked behind Aaron up the stairs, bracing him a little when he swayed under Aunt Harriett's dead weight. It was as if I was split into two. One of me pressed my two hands hard against the back of Aaron's shirt, which was damp and sticky from the sweat he'd raised carrying Aunt Harriett back to the house. Another of me was a basket case, thundering heart and a tiny little voice inside mewling, "No! No! No!"

Together, Aaron and I got the blue dress off and straightened her against the pillows with a cotton lace shawl over her thin bare shoulders. She didn't ever really come to, but every once in a while she jerked her head from side to side and moaned a little. I couldn't stand to look right at her without huge gulps of sobs rearing up against my throat. Aaron laid a cold wet cloth on her head just as we heard the screech of tires in the drive.

Aaron took the steps two at a time going down.

12
Choices

~~~~~~~

After Dr. Hollis went up to Aunt Harriett's room, I sat on the bottom step of the stairs and tried to force my mind away from what was going on up there. I had to scoot over and make room for Aaron to race by me to the kitchen for something. I had hardly settled again before I had to move to let him go back up.

There was another difference between movies and real life that I had never thought of before. Real life is cluttered up with a lot of details that don't really matter or move the action forward but just happen, getting between you and what you want to know. Movies strip all that stuff away, leaving the bones of the story bare like the limbs of a winter tree.

Aunt Harriett could die. She would be a rock in water the way Aaron said Geoff would be. The difference was how we would stand against that rushing water. She had said the shortest lives cast the longest shadows. After a while, I couldn't imagine feeling shadowed by Aunt Harriett's death at all. For one thing, I remembered how frustrated she had been to have to quit driving her car when she turned eighty. She was tired of being old and alone without Uncle Paris. Maybe she really wouldn't go away at all but only join the company of her ghosts, who were already as real to her as everybody except Aaron and me.

Aaron finally came down and stayed, limping back and forth across the hall. When the doctor came out of Aunt Harriett's room and started down to us, I had an instant sense of having seen all this before. I even recognized *where* I had seen it. In one, or several, old black-and-white movies.

[Candles—or oil lamps—flutter as the old doctor with grand moustaches comes slowly down the stairs. He is wearing a long-tailed coat with buttons at the waist and a collar that springs back from his throat. His tall hat and cane wait in the foyer below. He sets his fat black bag on the floor beside him as he pulls on his gloves. He doesn't meet anyone's eyes but speaks in a voice that seems to rise from the broad belly, straining the buttons of his vest. "I did everything within my power. She is now in the hands of God."]

Of course it wasn't like that at all. Dr. Hollis' wife had managed to catch up with him on his "daily five miles" and gotten him over there pretty fast. He was wearing a white sweat suit with orange stripes and he was as flat across the belly as I am. He didn't "descend" the stairs with the ponderous dignity of someone from Central Casting. He ran down the steps, two at a time, lightly, like the athlete that he is. His face, which had gleamed scarlet with sweat and heat when he arrived, had faded while he was upstairs with Aunt Harriett, leaving his skin only faintly colored by his early summer tan.

Then came the really glorious change in the script.

Instead of being gentle with us, Dr. Hollis exploded in anger. He couldn't know how ridiculous he looked, standing there in those oversized, overpriced running shoes, glaring at Aaron and me. His color came back in two furious red spots on his cheeks, making him look like a clown with his wig off. "I pulled her through that one," he barked at us. "No thanks to you two, but she's conscious again and breathing evenly. A few hours of sleep and she should be as good as new."

Aaron didn't wait to hear any more. He bounded past me toward the stairs, obviously intending to go up to Aunt Harriett. Dr. Hollis was too quick for him. He lunged and grabbed his arm as he passed, throwing him so badly off balance that Aaron had to catch at the newel post to keep from falling.

"Get back down here," Dr. Hollis ordered. "You are *both* going to listen to me now, whether you want to or not."

Aaron's face darkened the way it does when he's annoyed, but he stepped over to my side, his steady eyes hostile on Dr. Hollis' face.

"That is a very sick, very old woman," Dr. Hollis went on. He had regained enough control that he wasn't shouting, but his voice sounded strange, as if an unseen hand had caught it back in his throat and was squeezing the words out painfully one at a time.

I stared at him, recognizing that tone. That was the way Mom's voice had sounded out there in the dark of the back yard, right after the Wheatons had driven away Sunday night. Dr. Hollis was only lashing out at us because he had been scared. He had been caught helpless up there with Aunt Harriett, thinking she would die and he wouldn't be able to stop it.

His voice kept rising. "She should be in a hospital. You should have opted for the ambulance instead of slamming up the phone. If she had died up there just now, it would have been your fault. I want—"

Aaron shook his head. "I couldn't care less what you want. It's what Aunt Harriett wants that matters. You know how she feels about your swinging bottles and oxygen tanks and scurrying nurses. You have that notarized paper she signed. You know what her wish is on this!"

"Wish!" Dr. Hollis echoed, his flush deepening. "She drew up that document several years ago and you know it, because you were there when she signed it. How was she to know then that—"

Aaron startled both of us by laughing. "Go on," he goaded the doctor. "Finish *that* stupid sentence, too. 'How was she to know that she was going to die?' She knew. She's always known. She's seen more death as an amateur than you have as a professional. It's *her* life. She's run it on her own too long to let somebody else take over at the end."

Dr. Hollis must be about the same age as

Aaron, but the resemblance ends right there. Dr. Hollis is as fair as Aaron is dark, as well barbered as Aaron is shaggy. Dr. Hollis is taller but Aaron is more solid, thicker in the shoulders and chest from chopping wood for Aunt Harriett's fire, wrestling those old storm windows into place, and cutting the meadow grass with that big, long scythe.

The house sounds seemed to get louder to fill the silence that fell as the two men stared at each other. Apparently neither of them noticed. But the doctor wasn't family, and Aaron was concentrating too hard to hear thunder right then.

Maybe I wanted to hear Aunt Harriett's ghosts so much that I did. The captain's cane thumped on the upper right balcony as he walked his lonely vigil. Ida fingered the spinet keys in the library, and Uncle Paris moved from door to door along the upstairs hall. And I smiled.

Dr. Hollis dropped his eyes first. "I know what you're saying," he told Aaron, with a hint of apology in his tone. "But I still think the family should be warned. One of these emergencies will be her last. It would be a shame for a grand old lady like that to die alone." He shot a quick guilty glance at me, as if to apologize for speaking so bluntly in front of a child.

For once, that didn't even make me mad. The years were going to keep coming down on me whether I wanted them to or not. Hadn't I just been dragged, kicking and screaming, into being thirteen? The important thing was for me to remember how insulting it was to live in a world in which everybody tries to hide life from you. I *had* to remember so I wouldn't do it to any kids of my own.

"Don't worry about that," I told the doctor. Aaron looked at me, obviously startled because he's not used to my speaking up without being forced into it. "I *am* family, you know. And Aunt Harriett has never been alone for a minute in her life. By herself, maybe," I added quickly because that sounded so stupid. "By yourself is not the same as being alone."

I felt their eyes follow me as I started up the stairs.

When I first pushed the door open, I thought she was asleep. She was lying completely still with her arms loosely crossed on the top of the rose-colored coverlet. She heard me and spoke without opening her eyes. Right away I realized Dr. Hollis had given her some kind of medicine because her words came out sounding as if she had cotton in her mouth.

"Sorry about that," she said (Aaron's phrase). "I hope I didn't scare you young people."

I tugged at the cover, which was already plenty

neat enough. "It was Dr. Hollis you scared," I told her.

She opened her eyes and looked intently at me. "He'll be all right in a few years," she assured me. "He's got a lot of the old Doc in him. What happened out there?"

"I don't really know," I admitted, telling her how I had waited downstairs while Dr. Hollis examined her. "I think it was something like little blood vessels breaking in your head again, the way Aaron said they did before."

She was clearly concentrating, gripping her mind hard against the force of the medicine. "And I guess Aaron hauled me up here."

I nodded. "Like a sack of potatoes in a blue dress." Then, because everything works better if you can keep it light, I added, "Those humongous yellow boots added a nice touch."

She chuckled and groped for my hand. "You're all right, Emily Prentice. One of a kind." Her eyes drifted shut and she sighed. "That boy of Doc's shot me with something like the kick of a mule. Young fool!"

"He was scared," I reminded her.

"You weren't?" she asked.

"The music from Ida's spinet sounded like a lullaby," I told her.

She stared at me hard a minute before the bed started shaking from her laughter. After she'd settled back down and been still a long time, I started for the door. Her voice seemed to come from a long way away.

"Would you open that window a crack before you leave, honey? That feisty young cardinal has apparently finally got his very own song down pat. He's whooping it up in the black walnut tree and I can only half hear him through the glass."

With the window propped on a piece of kindling, a little breeze strayed in, carrying the bird's song so clearly you could hear every note. The sheer curtain blew in and out, pleating and straightening restlessly, the way Maudie fools with the hem of her apron when she is fretting. The air smelled of roses. That would be the multiflora hedge Aunt Harriett and Aaron had set out to give the little wild animals a safe place to hide from Rufus.

Halfway down the stairs, I smelled Rufus himself and knew Aaron had let him into the kitchen. Then I heard Aaron's voice—not any words, just the rhythm of his voice, interrupted now and then by a sharp bark. When the back screened door slammed, I knew he had carried a heaping washbasin of dog food out to the back walk for Rufus, who eats with so much gusto that he throws food everywhere. By the time I reached the kitchen, Aaron was back, washing his hands and frowning at the faucet.

He glanced at me.

"Asleep," I told him. "She looks fine, like always."

He grumbled something, then turned and wiped his hands on Maudie's apron.

With his back still to me, he filled the Blue Onion teapot from the tea kettle humming on the back burner. "That fop of a doctor and his hot water. We might as well use it."

Of course I hadn't been honest with Aunt Harriett about being scared. At least half of me had been scared spitless, but Aaron had been scared, too. The anger in his voice gave that away. He needed to ease up worse than he needed hot tea.

"I told Aunt Harriett how she looked when you hauled her upstairs," I said, sitting on the bench behind the kitchen table. "She laughed."

He looked shocked, then set out two mugs before sitting down across from me. "You are two of a kind, you and that old woman. You had me fooled for a long time. I used to think you were just all nose with nobody at home in that head."

Like the Amish doll, the Sunday Doll, up in my closet between the sweater stacks, staring without eyes into folded tissue paper. The first thing I was going to do when I got home was set that doll out. Give her the center of the shelf. And apologize to her. I'd been halfway convinced that she was some sort of a bad luck charm that started all the agony of the days just past. That was childish. All the problems—Geoff's, Jayne's, and my own angry rebellion—had been building up a long time and just happened to break through the sand into light at the same time. Even those weak little veins in Aunt Harriett's brain that were nudging her toward death had started weakening long before we set out for the orchard.

Once I got back home with Mom and Dad, who were trying to hang onto a kid already on the way to becoming a grownup, I was going to need that Sunday Doll out there to look at every day. Let her keep reminding me that my life was my own, that the face I turned to the world was mine to choose. Like Aunt Harriett. Like Aaron.

Aaron is comfortable with silence. He finished his tea, rose, and rinsed the mug out at the sink. "Guts," he said, with his back still to me. "You never blinked out there. Didn't you know we could have lost her?"

I shook my head. "I guess I don't much believe you ever lose people you love."

Upstairs, Aunt Harriett was sleeping, probably giving out a quick gusty snore every few breaths, the way she usually did. The house seemed awfully quiet. Even the ghosts of all those lives that had made Aunt Harriett what she was and were still making me what I was going to be were silent. All of us knew she needed her rest.

Then I remembered what I had discovered about movies and real life. There was nothing that Aaron and I could do right then to make the story come out right. We might as well get on with the cluttery little real-life things that make the difference.

"We aren't expecting any company to show off for," I reminded him. "How about we cook *all* that asparagus and eat it with melted butter for our supper?"

He grinned at me and reached up on the shelf for the steamer.

Mary Francis Shura has written over twenty books for young people. Born in Kansas, not far from Dodge City, the author has lived in many parts of the United States, including California and Massachusetts. Both of her parents came from early settler families of Missouri.

Aside from writing fiction for young readers and adults, Mary Francis Shura enjoys tennis, chess, reading, and cooking, especially making bread.

The mother of four grown children—Minka, Dan, Ali, and Shay—the author currently makes her home in the western suburbs of Chicago, in the village of Willow-brook.

Her most recent book is *Don't Call Me Toad!* *The Josie Gambit* is an ALA Notable. Two other titles, *Chester* and *Eleanor*, were selected for Children's Choices by the International Reading Association Children's Book Council Joint Committee. *The Search for Grissi* won the 1985 Carl Sandburg Literary Arts Award for Children's Literature.

91 - ||
92 - ||||
93 - |
94 - |||